"'Nameless' is a good man to walk you through the noir landscape."
—Marilyn Stasio, *New York Times Book Review*

"One of the best in the mystery-suspense field is Bill Pronzini."
—*Washington Post Book World*

"Pronzini makes people and events so real that you're living those explosive days of terror."
—Robert Ludlum

"Pronzini delivers breathtaking suspense."
—*San Francisco Examiner*

"'Nameless Detective' is a classic private-eye hero."
—*Chicago Sun-Times*

"One of the greatest-ever detective series."
—*Booklist* (starred review)

"Pronzini is the master of the shivery, spine-tingling, it-could-happen suspense story."
—*Publishers Weekly*

"An exceptionally skilled writer working at the top of his ability."
—*Denver Post*

"There is no living writer whose work more faithfully embodies the spirit of classic private-eye fiction than Bill Pronzini's."
—*Cleveland Plain Dealer*

SENTINELS

SENTINELS

A
"Nameless Detective"
Mystery

BILL PRONZINI

CARROLL & GRAF PUBLISHERS
NEW YORK

SENTINELS
A "NAMELESS DETECTIVE" MYSTERY

Carroll & Graf Publishers
An Imprint of Avalon Publishing Group Incorporated
161 William Street, 16th Floor
New York, NY 10038

First Carroll & Graf cloth edition 1996

First Carroll & Graf trade paperback edition 2002

Library of Congress Cataloging-in-Publication Data is available.

ISBN: 0-7867-1014-4

Printed in the United States of America
Distributed by Publishers Group West

For the Zimmermans
—Rod, Carolyn, and
my godsons, Patrick and Alex

SENTINELS

1

I probably would not have taken on the McDowell case if circumstances hadn't contrived to prod me into it. If I hadn't taken the case, then I wouldn't have been away from San Francisco for most of the last week in April. And if I hadn't been away from the city, and caught up in a different, highly volatile set of circumstances . . .

The old "what-if" game. Play it long enough and you can make yourself a little crazy.

Truth is, circumstances shape most things we do, nearly every day of our lives. Not just those in which we have a direct hand—the actions of strangers as well as people we know, that affect our lives in ways large and small, good or bad, known or unknown. The ripple effect. There's a theory I once heard: If someone were to invent a time machine and travel back into the dim past, to the Paleolithic era, say, and kill a prehistoric man or animal, or even crush a flower, the ripple effect of that single act through the centuries could conceivably alter the entire course of history. Alter it enough, in fact, so that the present would be nothing at all like it is now.

Sounds far-fetched, but I don't think it is. Consider this: You're driving to work and some idiot runs a red light at fifty and you narrowly manage to avoid a fatal collision. But what if you'd gotten up three seconds later that morning? *Three seconds.* If you had, you wouldn't have avoided the collision. If you had, you'd no longer be alive.

Circumstances.

And the old "what-if" game.

See what I mean about making yourself a little crazy if you play it long enough?

It was a missing persons case. Or to look at it the way I did when I first heard of Helen McDowell's problem, a worried mother job. I don't much like worried mother jobs; I'd had another one recently and it hadn't turned out well for any of the parties concerned. There's usually too much emotion involved, particularly when the missing person is an only child—a daughter, in this case—and the mother lives alone. Matters get exaggerated, blown out of proportion. Feelings run high. And the one who is liable to wind up caught in the middle is the detective, the outsider. Me.

So I was leery of the McDowell case, even if I did sympathize with what she was going through. My instincts said to turn her down, refer her to another agency. Easy enough over the phone; you're saying no to a disembodied voice. She wanted me to come over to Lafayette so we could discuss the details in person; she ran a boutique there and didn't want to leave for any length of time during business hours in case her daughter called, or the authorities called with news of the daughter. She was sure I understood—didn't I? I understood, all right. I should have said no anyway, and would have if it weren't for the circumstances.

The first was that I was out of the office when her call came in. My part-time assistant, Tamara Corbin, took it and the particulars. Tamara is feisty as well as a whiz with computers, and is not afraid to speak her mind on any subject. She is also a college student majoring in computer science at San Francisco State, and about the same age as Allison McDowell, the missing daughter. Sisterly empathy, therefore, for Allison—and for the mother.

"You've got to help her," Tamara said when I'd finished listening to the tape of her conversation with Mrs. McDowell. Taping all incoming and outgoing calls, hers and mine both, for future reference had been Tamara's idea, and a good one it was. So good and so logical that I felt inept for not having thought of it myself years ago. "I mean, this poor woman is half out of her head. Tries to hide it, but you can tell. She's got nobody else."

"She didn't say that."

"Didn't have to, did she? You're the man."

"Just like that, huh?"

"Far as I'm concerned."

"You don't mind if I talk to the woman myself before I make any decisions?"

"Go ahead, talk to her." Ms. Corbin fixed me with her brown stare—and that refers to eye color, not to the rich chocolate hue of her skin. "In person, not on the phone. And then you go ahead and find that missing girl."

The second circumstance was almost a coincidence. I was scheduled to deliver a subpoena in Walnut Creek at one that afternoon, and Walnut Creek, way out in Contra Costa county, is next door to Lafayette. I had to drive right by one to get to the other. And In the Mode, Helen McDowell's boutique, was in downtown Lafayette, two minutes off the freeway.

Third and fourth circumstances: This was a Monday and the only work I had lined up for the rest of the week was the subpoena delivery and a routine skip-trace. If I'd had the usual full workload, I could not have afforded to take four or five days away from the office; as things were, Tamara could handle the skip-trace just as well as I could. Better, thanks to her trusty Apple PowerBook. There was also the fact that I'd just lost out to one of the city's larger detective agencies on what promised to be a lengthy (and lucrative) investigation for the defense in a high-profile murder trial, a job I'd been counting on to pay a good percentage of the bills over the next few months. As a consequence, I was fretting more than usual about money.

The fifth and final and maybe most significant circumstance: I was in what Kerry calls my "tender frame of mind," tender

being a synonym for soft-hearted—and soft-headed. In that dis-
position I tend to lose perspective and respond to distress sig-
nals with disregard for my better judgment. The last time I'd
been "tender," round about April Fool's Day, I had become the
not-so-proud parent of a half-starved and flea-riddled kitten I'd
found foraging in the garbage cans behind my apartment building. One of its parents anyway. The kitten now lived in Kerry's
condo, since she was home more than I was; it had begun to
grow fat and sassy, and kept trying to sleep on me whenever I
spent the night there.

So I didn't say no to Helen McDowell any more than I'd said
no to the kitten. On the phone, after I'd listened to her outline
once again the central facts of her daughter's disappearance, I
said I'd stop by In the Mode around two o'clock and she could
fill me in on the details. I didn't commit myself beyond that, but
I might as well have. By agreeing to a face-to-face meeting I was
already committed. I wouldn't say no to her in person, either,
and I damned well knew it going in.

Lafayette, tucked into the low, rolling hills east of Oakland,
was born as a tiny farm center, began to grow rapidly in the
years following World War II, and by 1970 had earned dubious
status as an upscale bedroom community. Even so, it managed
to maintain most of its rural character. Like its west-side neighbor, Orinda, it is an upper-middle-class enclave catering to
those individuals who can afford to live comfortably and quietly
in homes on large tree-shaded lots that sell for a minimum of a
quarter-million and run to as much as eight times that for hillside estates.

The older section of downtown Lafayette has buildings dating
back to the turn of the century. Face-lifts and interior renova-
tion have kept them looking fresh without sacrificing any of
their old-fashioned charm. In the Mode was in one of these
dowagers, on a side street just off Mt. Diablo Boulevard. The

storefront was narrow and so was the store itself; every available space was tightly packed with articles of women's clothing and accessories, on floor and wall racks, in glass cases, on display cubes. The effect was not one of clutter, nor was the arrangement haphazard; it was all set out with an artist's eye for maximum sales appeal. The clothing ran to paisley prints, bright colors, sequins, and tasteful embroidery—the kind of stuff Kerry would probably have called casual chic. Half a dozen full-length mirrors placed at strategic intervals made the shop seem larger than it actually was.

There were no customers when I walked in a couple of minutes past two, just two middle-aged women talking quietly behind the sales counter. I knew immediately which of them was Helen McDowell. She was tallish, on the thin side, with light brown hair cut short; wearing a beige suit and a blue silk scarf. She was forty-five or so, but the facial baggage she carried that makeup couldn't hide, the drawn and pinched features, the worry that darkened her eyes, made her seem ten years older. It had been eight days since her daughter's disappearance; she and sleep, the way it looked, had been strangers most of that time.

I look exactly like what I am, so as soon as she saw me she murmured something to the other woman and came over to greet me. "Thanks so much for coming."

I nodded. "Still no word?"

"None. It's so frustrating . . . I'm at my wits' end."

"Is there someplace private we can talk?"

"My office. This way."

Her office was at the rear, not much more than a cubicle jammed with a desk, two chairs, articles of clothing, bundles, piled boxes. "I'm sorry for the mess," she said, "but we just don't have enough room here. I'd like to move to a larger location, but the rents in this area . . . Oh, God, you don't care about that. Neither do I right now."

There was nothing for me to say to that. On the desk was a framed photograph of a smiling young woman wearing a dark sweater and a string of pearls—formal head-and-shoulders portrait, and from the look of it, professionally taken. I gestured toward it. "Your daughter?"

"Yes, that's Allison." She picked it up, looked yearningly at the photo for a few seconds, bit her lip, and then handed it to me. "Taken about six months ago."

Allison McDowell appeared to be slender, almost slight. Pale blond hair worn long with a center part—maybe dyed, maybe not. Snub nose, high cheekbones, small mouth, almond-shaped brown eyes that gave her face a faint Asian cast.

"She's very attractive."

"Yes. Yes, she is."

I returned the photo, and as she sat in her chair she set it back on the desk, turning the frame so we could both see the smiling face. She cleared her throat before she said, "I don't remember how much I told you and your secretary on the phone. I'm afraid I'm not tracking very well . . . you'll have to excuse me."

Tamara Corbin would not have taken well to being called my "secretary"; but there wasn't any point in correcting Mrs. McDowell. I said, "It's all right. Why don't you just start again at the beginning."

"The beginning. Well, Allison is a junior at the University of Oregon. Studying architecture. That's not a common field for a woman, I'm sure you know that, but Allison isn't a common person in any way. I know that sounds like a mother's pride, but it's true. She's quite intelligent—her IQ is one twenty-five—and quite dedicated to her studies. Her grade point average is three point nine . . ."

When I nodded without speaking, she said, "I'm telling you all this because it's important that you know Allison is a serious young lady. Not frivolous or silly or boy-crazy, like some girls her age. She's concerned with women's issues, campus politics, environmental causes—an activist, though not in any disruptive way. Serious and responsible, that's my Allison. She wouldn't take it into her head to just . . . run off somewhere for more than a week without letting me know, especially not when I was expecting her home. She simply isn't capable of that sort of reckless behavior."

"It might not have been her idea," I said.

"Her new friend, you mean? Did I tell you about him?"

"Yes. You said you had the impression your daughter is serious about him. If she's in love . . ."

Mrs. McDowell was shaking her head. "No. That's why I told you what I just did about Allison. The Lassen County sheriff's captain I've been dealing with—his name is Fassbinder, Ralph Fassbinder—keeps harping on the idea that she and this young man of hers took it into their heads to run off together, elope or whatever. But he's wrong. I know my daughter. No matter how much in love she might be, it wouldn't change the way she is and always has been. She would never willingly worry me like this, hurt me . . . we're not just mother and daughter, we're best friends, we've always been extremely close . . . no. Something's happened—I know it, I can feel it, I . . ." She was becoming badly agitated and she realized it. She took several deep breaths; the effort it cost her to compose herself was palpable. "I'm sorry," she said at length. "I promised myself I wouldn't become emotional, and I won't."

I said gently, "You don't need to apologize to me, Mrs. McDowell."

"Thank you. But I want to be as businesslike as possible."

"About this new boyfriend. You don't know anything about him, not even his name?"

"Nothing at all. The first I knew Allison was seeing someone new was when she called from Eugene ten days ago."

"Just what did she say?"

"That she was taking a few days off from her job—she works part-time in a bookstore—and driving home with a friend she wanted me to meet."

"A male friend."

"Not even that, but I assumed it was."

"Why?"

"Her tone of voice. She was excited, bubbly . . . I hadn't heard her quite so animated in some time. The inflection when she said the word 'friend' . . . well, if you were a woman, a mother, you'd understand."

"Did you ask the friend's name?"

"Yes. She said it was a surprise."

"A surprise?"

"Allison loves surprises. Springing them as well as being on the receiving end. Ever since she was a little girl. It's . . . she has a mischievous side, you see."

"How do you mean, mischievous?"

"When I said she was serious, a serious young woman, I didn't mean to give you the impression that she's that way all the time, that she doesn't have a sense of humor. She's fun-loving too. And she can be impish at times. I think that's why she didn't tell anyone, not even her roommates, about this new young man."

"Sorority roommates?"

"No. She doesn't belong to a sorority. She and three other girls share a house off campus. I spoke to two of them, Karyn Standish and Chris Hammond. They were as surprised she was seeing someone new as they were about her dis—about her not arriving home as planned."

"She did tell them she was driving down to the Bay Area?"

"Yes, but she let them think she was making the trip alone."

"Didn't they think that was odd? Her leaving school so suddenly?"

"Allison didn't leave school. It was Easter break week at the university."

"Oh, I see." I paused because she was looking at the photo again. Her eyes were moist. Don't cry, I thought, don't do that to either of us. She didn't; her control now was under a tight rein. "You believe Allison kept the new boyfriend a secret from her roommates for the same reason she kept it from you? So she could surprise them at some point?"

"It's the sort of harmless little game she loves to play."

Maybe not so harmless after all. But I didn't put voice to the thought. I asked, "Has she ever done anything like that before? Been . . . impish about her relationships with men?"

"No," Helen McDowell said. "That's what makes me so certain this new young man is someone special."

"How special? Engagement, marriage?"

"Entirely possible. Allison can be impulsive now and then, and her commitments tend to be deep and intense. With the right man, someone she considers a soulmate . . . yes, she's quite capable of falling in love quickly and just as quickly deciding to marry."

"But she'd want your blessing first."

"My blessing would be important to her. Whether she got it or not, she'd want me to know what she intended and to meet the young man before she did it."

"You're sure of that."

"Absolutely. As I told you, Allison and I are very—"

The telephone rang. The sudden eruption of sound made us both jump. Helen McDowell sucked in her breath, a rasping sound almost as loud as the phone bell, and went after the instrument the way a cat pounces on a piece of raw meat. Private line, I thought, not the one for store business.

"Yes? Hello?" Her face, in those first couple of seconds, was a study in naked hope. But then, as she listened, the hope shriveled and her face sagged, as if drawn downward by invisible weights. Her voice was flat when she said, "No, Deirdre, not a word yet . . . It's all right, dear. I know you're worried too. . . . Yes, as soon as I know anything. Promise . . . I will. Yes. Bye for now."

She replaced the receiver slowly, almost carefully. "That was Deirdre Collins, Allison's best friend. Her best friend all through high school, I should say. They're not as close as they used to be, but then, distance does that to friendships."

"She knew your daughter was coming home?"

"Allison called her before she left Eugene. But she didn't say

11

anything more to Deirdre about her young man than she did to me."

I'd been making notes on a pad I carry and I glanced over them before I spoke again. After Allison's name I had written: *Intelligent, dedicated, concerned, responsible, fun-loving, mischievous, secretive, impulsive, loves surprises, prone to making deep and intense commitments.* Allison McDowell was an uncommon person, all right. Uncommonly complex. She and her mother were close, but how well can even a mother know her daughter? Particularly a daughter as complicated and evidently headstrong as Allison.

I said, "So she and her friend left Eugene on the morning of Friday, the twelfth. Is that right?"

"Yes."

"In Allison's car."

"An old MG, not very reliable—I've been after her to trade it in on a newer model. But she loves that old wreck. Even when it broke down on Saturday, she wouldn't hear of getting rid of it."

"It broke down where?"

"Outside a little town called Creekside. Off Highway 395, halfway between Susanville and Alturas."

That was in the northeastern corner of California, where it joins Oregon on the north and Nevada on the east—a fairly remote part of the state. "They went that way, to Three ninety-five, for what reason? The trip down from Eugene is a lot faster on Highway Five."

"I know," Helen McDowell said. "But when Allison called that Saturday evening, she said they'd decided to take a more scenic route. Neither she nor her friend had ever been over that way and they wanted to see what the country was like. Impulsive, you see?"

"What else did she say on the phone?"

"That the MG had broken down on the highway and they'd had it towed to a garage in Creekside. The man at the garage thought he could have it fixed by ten Sunday morning. If the car didn't break down again, she said, they'd be here—in Lafayette—by Monday evening at the latest." Mrs. McDowell drew a heavy breath. "That was the last I heard from her."

"She was in Creekside when she called?"

"At the only motel. The Northern Comfort Cabins."

"How did she sound?"

"Happy. Very happy. She even . . . she made a little joke. 'Having wonderful time, Mom, glad you're not here.' "

"As far as you know, she and the friend left Creekside as scheduled—around ten Sunday morning."

"Yes. That was the last anyone saw of them, when they drove away from the garage and out to the highway."

"Who saw them then? The garageman?"

"The owner, yes. His name is Maxe, Art Maxe."

"You spoke to him personally?"

"That's right."

"Who else up there?"

"A Mr. Bartholomew, the owner of the motel."

"Did you ask either man about Allison's companion?"

"Both. They weren't very forthcoming. About all they'd say is that he was male. Bartholomew said he didn't know the young man's name because Allison had registered in her name only and paid with her credit card."

"Did you get an impression of why neither Maxe nor Bartholomew was forthcoming?"

"It wasn't that they were unfriendly, just reticent. The way people in small towns are when they deal with strangers, especially over the phone."

"They must've given Captain Fassbinder a description of the man, even if they couldn't supply his name. He'll be identified eventually."

"Yes, but when? It's been four days since Allison was officially listed as missing, and Fassbinder hasn't bothered to call and give me any sort of update. Before I phoned you this morning, I called him and he *still* wouldn't tell me anything. All he'd say is that he's investigating."

"That's standard procedure, Mrs. McDowell. Police agencies don't like to pass along inconclusive or uncorroborated information."

"But, my God, four days! How competent is the Lassen Sheriff's Department, really? How hard are they trying? Allison and her young man didn't just drop off the face of the earth—they weren't abducted by aliens, for heaven's sake. It's maddening. . . ."

I let all of that pass. Four days sounded like a long time, but it wasn't; missing persons investigations are methodical time-users. And the fact is, though I wasn't about to tell it to Helen McDowell, it's a relatively low-priority police matter. Lassen County, where Allison was last seen and therefore the police agency with jurisdiction, would have refused to list her as officially missing until the Thursday after she was last seen—the mandatory seventy-two hours in cases where there is no evidence of foul play. Prior to that, all they'd have done was to take Allison's name and the license number of her MG and put out a statewide stop-and-check order. Even now, with Allison on the books as a missing person, Mrs. McDowell was right—Captain Fassbinder probably *wasn't* expending a lot of effort on the case. You could understand it from the authorities' point of view: Kids were liable to do all sorts of crazy things on a whim, with little or no consideration for their parents, and every police agency has been burned too many times by false alarms. Give them something definite to go on, such as a hint of a felony crime, and they'd bust their humps. Until, if, and when that happened, Fassbinder would continue to spend most of his time frying bigger fish.

One of the things Helen McDowell wanted from me was reassurance. But I was not going to lie to her; the truth, or at least a softened version of the truth, was less unkind. I said, "Mrs. McDowell, I have to be honest with you. I don't know that I can do much the authorities aren't already doing. I'm only one man. And California is a big state. Allison and her friend could've vanished anywhere within a radius of several hundred miles, could be anywhere at all right now—"

"I know that. I *know* all that. But you could go to Creekside, try to trace them from there. Couldn't you? I thought of doing it myself, but I'm not a detective, I wouldn't know where to start or what questions to ask. That's what I'd like to hire you to do, go to Creekside and try, just . . . try. Will you do that for me, for my daughter? Please?"

I said yes, all right, I would try.

What else could I say? Circumstances had already committed me.

2

It was nearly five when I got back to the office. Tamara was still there, tapping away industriously on her Apple PowerBook, a frown of concentration wrinkling her round face. She'd taken to wearing what for her was conservative clothing to the office—blouses and slacks, even a skirt now and then. The green blouse and beige slacks she had on today were a far cry from her outfit the first time I'd set eyes on her last fall: purple and yellow tie-dyed scarf over her close-cropped hair, too-large man's plaid shirt, rumpled and ripped orchid-colored pants, green strap sandals revealing a gaggle of silver and gold toe rings. What she'd called "the grunge look." And she'd had, back then, a pretty grungy attitude to go with it.

The attitude had been racially defensive, snotty, and loaded with misconceptions about both private investigative work and the motivations of an upper-middle-aged Italian man in wanting to hire a twenty-year-old African American woman. We'd clashed hard enough to throw sparks at that first meeting. I not only hadn't hired her, I'd given her a dose of her own nastiness and sent her packing.

That would have been the end of it, except that underneath all the racial baggage she was lugging around, she was a good person. Intelligent, sensitive, owner of a caustic sense of humor, and quick to learn from her mistakes. She'd called a day later to apologize, which prompted me to give her a second-chance interview; and the Tamara Corbin who showed up for that one—better dressed, much less adversarial—had impressed me enough to hire her on a trial basis. I hadn't regretted the decision; on the contrary, it was one of the best business decisions I'd made in years. She reorganized my bookkeeping and filing, established a simplified billing system, conducted computer information searches and made the skiptraces and insurance background checks that were my bread and butter much easier to complete, answered the phone and dealt with potential clients when I was away from the office. For her part, even though most of the work was routine and unexciting, she'd taken to it with considerably more enthusiasm than either of us anticipated—so much so that she'd surprised me a couple of weeks ago by saying that the detective business might be a career option for her.

The blotter on my desk, I noticed, was empty except for its decorative polyglot of stains: ink, coffee, Liquid Paper, and others too obscure to identify. "No messages?" I said.

"Well, there were a couple of calls."

"From?"

"Bert Horowitz at Standard Armored Car. About that preemployment screening job we did for him last month."

"Some problem with it? The guy checked out . . ."

"No problem. He said we underbilled them."

"*Under*billed?"

"By a hundred bucks," Tamara said. "He's putting through another check to cover. You believe it?"

"The last honest man."

"Too bad all our clients aren't like him. Abe Melikian, number one."

"Good old Abe." Melikian was a bail bondsman who bitched about every expense account item and invariably took a full ninety days to pay up. "Tell me the other call was good news too."

"Wish I could."

"It wasn't?"

"Could be, but not business. Barney Rivera."

Small surprise. "What'd he want?"

"Personal, the man said. Nothing urgent. He'll call again."

Terrific. Barney Rivera, chief claims adjuster for Great Western Insurance. Roly-poly, jellybean-popping womanizer. Smart guy with a smart mouth and a bent sense of humor tainted by a streak of cruelty. We'd been pretty good friends until about a year ago. Kerry and I had been having some personal problems and Barney had exacerbated them—intentionally and maliciously, in my opinion. Things had been cool between us since. For years he'd thrown eight or ten jobs per annum my way— Great Western farmed out its investigative work to independent contractors like me—but that number had dropped off to two in the past six months. I hadn't heard from him at all in more than three months; and I'd picked up rumors that he was giving all of the company's claims work to Eberhardt, my former partner and current competitor. I had just about written off Barney the Needle and Great Western, and now he'd surfaced again. Only not for a business reason. And sure as hell not to apologize: Barney never apologized to anybody. Most likely he wanted something from me—information, a favor . . .

". . . that woman's case?"

Tamara, I realized, had quit tapping and was fixing me with her brown stare. "Sorry, what'd you say?"

"You take that woman's case? Mrs. McDowell."

"I took it."

"Good. I knew you would."

"Good for us, maybe. Chances are, she's throwing her money away. I doubt there's much I can do."

"What happened to the daughter, you think?"

"Hard to judge. Nothing good, or some trace of her would've turned up by now. I don't suppose you'd care to hear the details of her disappearance?"

She favored me with a half-smile. They used to have a sharp cynical edge, those half-smiles of hers; now the cynicism was tempered by more favorable emotions. "Mellowing," she'd have called it. I called it "maturing."

She said, "Do bears do the nasty in the great outdoors?"

"I hope I never get close enough to find out."

"Makes two of us. I'm listening."

I gave her a rundown of my interview with Helen McDowell. She didn't interrupt; she was an attentive listener, one of the qualities a good detective needs to have. She had others too—an instinctive feel for which facts were important and which weren't, advanced problem-solving abilities, and healthy doses of insight and imagination. I'd taken to confiding in her on cases where I felt a perspective different from mine would be beneficial.

"Sure doesn't sound good," she said when I'd finished. "That girl's the type got her head on straight, if what her mama told you is right. She wouldn't've run off with the mystery man. Uh-uh, not Allison."

"Even though she's mischievous, loves surprises?"

"No way. That type plays little controlled games, not ones that're off the wall. Airheads run off with a guy, mainly so they can screw their selfish little brains out. Allison's no airhead."

"So what's your take on the situation?"

"No sense speculating when you don't have enough facts. Isn't that what you always say?"

"Go ahead and speculate anyway."

"Well, something must've happened to her," Tamara said. "Could be any damn thing if it happened to Mr. Mystery too. Accident, they got lost somewhere, they picked up the wrong kind of hitchhiker."

"Uh-huh."

"But if it was to just her alone—could be she picked the wrong dude to fall in love with. Lot of crazies out there, pretending to be normal. Start something with a girl, get her away someplace, do their sick thing, and more times than not, nobody ever finds out what went down. Man, I hope that's not it. But all the secrecy, Allison not even telling her mama his name . . ."

"You mean it could've been his idea, not hers. The secrecy."

"Right. And she went along on account of her love for sur-prises."

"One fact argues against that scenario," I said.

"You mean the people in Creekside who saw him?"

"That's it. The authorities have his description by now."

"Wouldn't matter if she's never found. Or if he's Mr. Average and a traveler and nobody can find him."

I nodded. She'd touched on most of the problems that had been bothering me. "So you see what I'm up against," I said. "Plenty of possibilities, most of them bad, and not many defi-nite facts. And only one starting point that'll like as not turn out to be a dead end."

"Creekside."

"Creekside," I agreed.

"You gonna drive or fly up there?"

"Drive. It's not much more than a wide place in the road and out in the middle of nowhere. Nearest airport is Susanville, and it's bound to be too small for any regularly scheduled commer-cial flight."

"Maybe you could get that detective friend of yours, Sharon McCone, to fly you up. She's a pilot, right? Got her own plane, keeps it over in Oakland?"

"Sure, she's a pilot, but the plane belongs to her significant other and he uses it for his own business. And Sharon's ex-panded her operations—she's away a lot of the time herself. And I wouldn't bother her for a favor like that even if she weren't a friend. I can get to Creekside almost as fast in my own car."

"Scared to fly in one of those little planes, huh?"

"You know something, Ms. Corbin? Sometimes you're too smart for your own good. All right, I admit it. The one time I went up in a plane as small as hers—a 'matchbox with wings,' she calls it—there was a lot of turbulence and I almost needed a diaper."

She laughed. "I hear you. Wouldn't catch me flying in one either."

Helen McDowell had given me two color photos of her daughter, both head-and-shoulders portraits from the same batch as the framed one on her desk. I passed one to Tamara for inclusion in the McDowell case file.

"So that's Allison."

"That's Allison. Taken about six months ago."

She studied the photo for several seconds. "Pretty," she said, and then, "Funny. I knew a white girl once, looked a little like her. Down on the Peninsula."

"Did you?"

"When I was in high school. She married a plumber."

"A plumber."

"Yeah. He came over to her house to fix her folks' pipes. Ended up fixing hers instead. Laid some pipe on her and clogged her drain, you know what I'm saying?"

I didn't at first. Then I sorted it out. "Got her pregnant so they had to get married."

"Knocked up big as a boiler."

"So what's your point?"

"Point?"

"About this girl you knew and Allison McDowell."

"Isn't one. They looked a little alike, that's all."

"I thought you were making a point."

"Well, I wasn't." She gave me one of those generation-gap looks. "You know," she said, "you and my old man ought to get together. He thinks everything has to have a point too. Must be a cop thing." Her father, Darryl Corbin, was a lieutenant of detectives with the Redwood City police.

"A cop thing and a mature guy thing," I said. "But we don't *think* everything has to have a point, we *wish* everything had one."

"So what's your point?" she asked, deadpan.

I laughed in spite of myself. "Definitely too smart for your own good."

"I know it. Horace says I'm one of a kind."

"He won't get any argument from me." Horace was her "hardman," which I presumed meant boyfriend, lover, soulmate. I hadn't discussed the term with her because I was afraid she'd provide me with a too-precise definition. He stood about six two, weighed around 240, and had the general demeanor of Mean Joe Greene on game day. He was an honor student at S.F. State, majoring in music appreciation, and was also studying to be a concert cellist at the Conservatory of Music. "How is Horace these days?"

"He's cool. Picking me up at five-fifteen." She glanced at her watch. "Oh, man, it's that now. He'll be downstairs and you know he doesn't like to wait."

I poked my chin in the direction of her computer. "Go ahead and log off or shut down or whatever it is you do with that thing."

"Nothing else you need?"

"Not today."

She did whatever it is she does to darken and disconnect the PowerBook, folded it up into its self-contained carrying case. "When you leaving for Creekside?" she asked then.

"Tomorrow morning, early."

"Well, I'll be in Wednesday and Thursday, same as usual. Got a couple of hours free on Friday morning, too, if you want me to come in then."

"Fine. I'll check in when I can."

At the door she said, "You find Allison, okay? Or at least what happened to her."

"If I can."

"Not just for her mama's sake. If she's alive, she's somebody deserves to have a life. Design buildings, work for causes, marry a plumber or her mystery man if he's cool—whatever. You hear what I'm saying?"

"Loud and clear. You wouldn't be making a point after all, would you?"

The half-smile again. "I guess maybe I am at that. Be smart now," she said, which meant that I should take care of myself, and out she went to brighten the evening of her budding concert cellist.

Home, for Kerry and me, is a two-sided proposition. Before we'd tied the knot we had made the decision that each of us maintain our separate residences. She had bought her apartment when her building on Diamond Heights went condo a few years ago, and I'd had my Pacific Heights flat—low rent, thanks to a benevolent landlord—for so long I could barely remember the other places in the city that I'd lived prior to it. So neither of us cared to give up one in favor of the other. Besides which, we were both set in our ways, both independent to a fault, both in need of a certain amount of privacy. The privacy factor was particularly important when one or the other of us was caught up in a difficult work schedule.

The arrangement, as unconventional as it was, probably would have caused trouble in most marriages; for us, it served as a bond of trust that made our relationship even more solid. Most weeks we spent five or six nights and the entire weekend together, more often at Kerry's condo than at my flat because she has a bigger bed (you can make of that what you like) and more space for her wardrobe and personal effects, and because it's easier for her to do the work that she regularly brings home from her office. She's a creative director at one of the city's larger ad agencies, Bates and Carpenter—the kind of job where the image you project, how you look and dress, is almost as important as how skillful you are at creating a selling ad layout. Kerry claims the bathroom in my flat is too dark and has what she calls "fun-house mirrors" so that she can never get her makeup on properly. I'm sure she's right. My craggy old phiz looks a hell of a lot less tolerable to my critical eye in her brightly lit bathroom mirror than it does in my shadowy one.

Tonight was one of our nights at the condo, so I drove straight up to Diamond Heights after I closed the office. Her building is on a steep street called Gold Mine Drive. On the plus side it offers one of the best views of the city; on the minus side, underground parking is limited to one car per unit and street parking, also limited, can be a pain in the ass. I got lucky this evening, though the lone free space half a block downhill was narrow and I had to do some jockeying back and forth to squeeze my car into it. It wasn't until I was done squeezing that I noticed the car parked behind mine, a butterscotch-hued Mercedes 560SL.

Uh-oh, I thought.

You don't see many Mercedes sport jobs painted that color; the only one I'd ever seen belonged to Paula Hanley, a friend of Kerry's who owned an interior design company and was a client of Bates and Carpenter's. Paula was all right, and we got on well enough most of the time, but she made me uncomfortable. What little sense of humor she had was bizarre, she was overly analytical, and she thought she knew what was best for everybody and consequently kept trying to manipulate and change other people's lives. These less-than-endearing traits were part of the reason she'd gone through three husbands and was working on a fourth, a poor tubby little chiropractor named Andrew. The other part had to do with a magnetic attraction to every screwball new fad, fancy, and ism that came along. She was always trying to talk Kerry into joining one of her harebrained new pursuits. So far Kerry, who was more practical than adventurous, had resisted. But it worried me that one of these days Paula would wear down her resistance and then poor tubby Andrew and I would finally have something significant in common.

So was Paula here tonight on business or on a fresh mission? On a mission, like as not; she usually reserved business matters for her office or Kerry's, and she'd been between fads, fancies, and isms longer than usual. Hooked into a new one, sure as hell, I thought fatalistically.

I steeled myself and went in to find out more than I would ever want to know about Paula Hanley's latest dementia du jour.

3

S_{ex}.

And didn't that just figure?

I could hear Paula gabbling as soon as I opened the door. She and Kerry were in the living room, at the opposite end of the apartment, but she might have been standing next to me yelling in my ear. She had one of those rare voices that indiscriminately ranges up and down the register from a deep-throated low to a piercing high, depending on her subject matter, mood, level of excitement, and intake of wine. The more animated she got, the more her voice took on a kind of breathless, fire-whistle shrillness. It hadn't reached that level yet tonight, but it was edging in that direction. She must've been a squealing bundle of fun in bed—one of the reasons, no doubt, that she'd gone through so many husbands, all of whom were now surely hearing-impaired. And if that's a sexist remark, Kerry gets the blame: She was its originator, not me.

". . . not exaggerating, Kerry, *The Holy Sexual Communion* is absolutely the most wonderful book I've ever read. It's so enlightening, so stimulating . . . so *profound.* It changed my entire outlook on love and marriage and human relationships, and if you read it and absorb its message, it will change yours too. Take the concept of 'high sex,' for instance. I mean, Andrew and I, well, we thought we had a perfectly satisfactory sex life right from the first, but after we read *The Holy Sexual Communion* and began attending Alida's workshops, we realized that all we'd been doing was going through the motions,

2 7

so to speak. What we have now, with our energy bodies in total harmony, is *so* much more intense and spiritual. . . ."

There was more, no doubt a lot more, but I didn't hear it except as background noise. I had one arm out of my coat, when a streak of black and tan fur shot around the corner from the kitchen and launched itself at me from about five feet away. I tried to catch it one-handed, missed, and it slammed into my right leg thigh-high with enough force to pitch me backward a step. Razor-sharp claws sank into my flesh; it was like being stabbed with a dozen needles all at once. Manfully I managed not to scream. The fur ball hung there, firmly anchored, looking up at me out of huge amber-colored eyes and making a sound like an electric grinder.

How can you get upset with something that weighs less than three pounds and gazes at you with such soulful adoration? I reached down and disengaged him gently from my bleeding leg. He snuggled in against my chest, making even louder rumbling noises, as if I were a blood relative instead of a primary provider of 9 Lives and Kitty Litter. "Cat," I said, "you really are well named," which he took as a cue to raise his head and adore me some more.

Right, I thought. When Kerry first came up with the name for him, I considered it silly. Not as silly as Fufu or Precious or some of the other saccharine things people call their felines, but silly enough for me to try to talk her out of it. She remained adamant. "It's perfect," she said. "It's what he is, isn't it?"

I couldn't argue with that, then or now. There really wasn't a better or more appropriate handle for the furry little bunco artist than Shameless.

I set him on the floor. He wound himself around my legs while I finished shedding my coat; then he went charging ahead of me as I limped down the hall into the living room.

Paula was still holding court, perched cross-legged on the couch, talking with her long-fingered hands as well as her crimsoned mouth. She wore black velour slacks and a chartreuse blouse that clashed violently with her lipstick and her lemon-yellow perm. She had a reputation as one of the city's most stylish home designers, and an annual income to back it up, but she couldn't decorate herself worth a hoot. Kerry, on the other hand, not only knows how to dress but always manages to look fresh and unrumpled at any hour of the day. Cream-colored suit and a blouse the shade of old port wine today, her long legs encased in a pair of sheer nylons. She was in her chair with her shoes off and her feet pulled up, which suited me fine; she has the sexiest feet of any human being on this planet. Sexy greenish chameleon eyes and a pretty hot neck too, especially where it curves up into the short auburn hair at the nape.

When Paula saw me she paused long enough in her monologue to draw a breath. This gave Kerry time to smile at me and say, "Hi, guy. You look tired."

"I am tired. And I can't stay long—my wife's expecting me. Hello, Paula."

"Hello yourself. What happened to your leg?"

"What? Oh. Shameless. He keeps using me as a scratching post." I went over to give Kerry a kiss. "We've got to have him declawed."

"That's not good for a cat," Paula said. "Cats need their claws, even housebound cats. It's not natural to have them removed."

"It's also not natural for me to walk around with blood dripping down my leg."

"Did he really scratch you that bad?" Kerry asked. "There's iodine in the bathroom. . . ."

"Later. I think the bleeding's stopped."

I resisted an urge to nibble the hair on her neck, avoided any more eye contact with her bare feet, and lowered my hams into my chair. Immediately Shameless jumped onto my lap and conned me into massaging his ears.

Paula's face, I noticed while I massaged, was flushed—partly from the excitement generated by her latest mania and partly from the effects of the wine she and Kerry had been drinking. A nearly empty glass stood on the end table beside her, and if I knew Paula, it wasn't her first. Next to the glass lay a small, slender hardcover book with a silver dust jacket that had *The Holy Sexual Communion* and the single author's name Alida splashed across it in dark purple.

The Hanley eyes, a little glazed from wine and fervor, were on me and had been ever since I'd walked in. They were a kind of off-amber color similar to Shameless's, just as round and also slightly ophthalmic, and whenever she watched me like that I got the uncomfortable sensation that I was being analyzed. The same sort of analysis a scientist might give a mildly interesting bug.

"You seem tense," she said.

"Pardon?"

"Tense. Your body language—it's sending messages of tension."

"Sort of like Western Union, you mean?"

She stared at me in a puzzled way: the bug had made sounds the scientist didn't understand. "I don't understand," she said.

"He was making a joke," Kerry said.

"Oh. A joke. Well, it must be the tension. What you should do after I leave is to give him a massage. You know, the kind I was telling you about—his back and arms with warm oil."

"Warm oil," I said. "What kind? Pennzoil, or will WD-40 do?" Paula brings out the worst in me.

"*Very* tense," she said.

Kerry said, "We're not much for massages. . . ."

"But that's just the point." Paula waved an arm and almost knocked over her wineglass. This made her aware of the glass; she drained it before she went on. "The whole idea of the tantric experience, the holy tantric communion, is for couples to expand their horizons. Learn new shared pleasures, teach other joys greater and more lasting than the fleeting orgasm. It's the one true path to enlightenment and bliss, to spiritual oneness."

I made the mistake of asking, "What're you talking about, Paula?"

"New Age tantra, of course."

"What's New Age tantra?"

"You've never heard of it? Really?"

"Really. What is it, besides some kind of new sex thing?"

She looked appalled. "New? Thing? The techniques of New Age tantra are derived from a meditative tradition founded in India fifteen hundred years ago."

"Yeah, huh?"

"Absolutely. In those days the rituals were held in secret because they went against established Buddhist and Hindu dogma. Devotees consumed taboo foods such as meat, drank alcohol, chanted sacred syllables, visualized gods and goddesses in symbolic sexual union during meditation, and copulated with one partner after another."

"Pretty kinky."

"Kinky? No, it was *spiritual.* The main difference between the old form and New Age tantra is that we're taught how to achieve ultimate intimacy with just *one* other person. A domestic and less religious version of the old teachings, although spirituality is still the core. New Age tantra is the antithesis of the free-love, noncommitment seventies, the autoerotic experimentation of the eighties. It's not only the perfect form of lovemaking for the monogamous, AIDS-aware nineties, it's what all human sexuality should evolve into—a holy communion, a rite of passage through the multifaceted changes of life and togetherness."

She was on a roll again. With each new sentence—quoted more or less verbatim, I'd have been willing to bet, from *The Holy Sexual Communion*—her voice rose another octave. The zealot's glaze made her eyes shine. She ran both hands through her hair, yanking at it as if she might be getting ready to snatch out handfuls by the roots; she didn't go that far, but she did succeed in creating an unintentional new 'do, a sort of New Age fright-wig style.

"It's not just sex," she said, "it goes far beyond simple physical connection. Closeness, intimacy, spirituality—that's what tantra teaches us. Pure love in which orgasm is truly nonessential. What you and your mate create together is a sacrament that brings you closer to God as well as to each other. You see?"

I saw, all right. I said, "How do you do it?"

"Do it? Do what?"

"Create this sacrament. Reach tantric Nirvana with your mate."

"By deemphasizing *sex*. Weren't you listening?"

"Deemphasizing sex. Uh-huh. You have sex by deemphasizing it." I glanced at Kerry. "Make sense to you?"

She said, "Well, in principle. The physical act isn't what's important. The emphasis is in finding ways to please your mate spiritually and emotionally as well as physically, which allows you to feel greater pleasure and closeness. Isn't that right, Paula?"

"Absolutely," Paula said. Somehow the second syllable came out a few decibels higher than the others, as if she were trying to imitate the whistle of a teakettle. Came pretty close too. "And in order for the ultimate connection to be made, you have to create the proper atmosphere. Preparations are vital."

"What sort of preparations?" I asked.

"Oh, there are many different techniques. We learn to use variations of all in sequence and harmony, in order to awaken the god and goddess in ourselves."

"Sort of a tantric version of foreplay."

"Yes! The last time Andrew and I had our morning prayer— that's what our lovemaking has become for us now, what Alida calls a morning prayer, even though we usually do it in the evening—the last time, he began by making an altar on the bureau of our chamber, surrounding a photograph of me with flowers. Roses and camellias, my favorites. Then he massaged my back and arms with warm scented oil. Then we sat facing each other on pillows before our statue of Buddha, and practiced full-body cuddling for a time, breathing slowly and gazing deep into each other's eyes. When we were both totally relaxed, totally *connected,* we sipped wine and fed each other dates and nuts—"

"Nuts," I said, and Kerry reached over to poke my arm. Paula didn't seem to notice.

"—in order to appease our physical hunger while our spiritual need sharpened and expanded. Then I chanted softly to him as he beat on his elkskin drum—"

"His what?"

"—chanted the words 'My body is the body of the Goddess,' and at that point my own goddess awakened both physically and spiritually. I *was* the Goddess. We drank wine while he stroked the plastic wand in my glass and I fondled my yoni puppet. Soon we were ready for—"

"Wait a minute," I said. "Yoni puppet?"

Kerry laid a warning hand on my arm. She said to Paula, "Um, maybe you'd better not get too explicit," but by then Paula had dragged her purse onto her lap and was hauling something out of it.

"This," she said, and held it up in all its bizarre splendor.

It was long and round and hollow and sort of furry at one end. It was made out of black velvet and pink silk. It looked like nothing so much as a giant, anatomically correct—

"My God!" I said.

"Isn't it beautiful?"

"It's a . . . it's a . . ."

"Valley of bliss," she said.

"Valley of . . . what?"

"That's the tantric name for it. Valley of bliss."

"Put it away!"

"Why? It's nothing to be ashamed of. How can there be shame in a woman's valley of bliss? Or in a man's wand of light?"

"A man's—"

"Wand of light. Once Andrew and I reached mutual harmony in our energy bodies, he illuminated my valley of bliss with his wand of light and we began the slow ascent to pure ecstasy. He was amazing that night. We moved our arousal up our spines to our brains, achieved a psychic eruption of enlightenment and bliss. Neither of us had a *physical* orgasm, yet we were both more fulfilled than if we had. Before we found tantra and began sharing our new sacrament, Andrew always had a problem with premature—"

"Stop already." I hoisted myself out of the chair, dislodging Shameless, who gave an indignant yowl and went bounding off across the room. I made eye contact with Kerry. She didn't seem embarrassed or put off by the explicit sex talk; in fact, she had her hand up to her mouth and seemed to be hiding a smile or stifling a laugh.

"What's the matter with you?" Paula asked me. Her voice had gone down-register again. The eye glaze had faded too; she stared up at me with a mixture of condescension and disapproval. "I didn't realize you were so prudish."

I said, "I'm not prudish."

Kerry said, "He's not prudish."

"Old-fashioned, then." Paula waved the yoni thing with what I took to be malicious emphasis. "Sexually repressed."

"Get that thing out of my sight, will you?"

"You know, you're the first man who ever said *that* to me. Most men—"

"I'm not most men."

"Well, that's obvious."

"He isn't sexually repressed," Kerry said.

"That's for damn sure," I said.

"He isn't? Then why does he act as if he is?"

"Talking explicitly about sex makes him uncomfortable, that's all. A lot of men are like that, Paula."

"Oh, I know they are. Andrew was a bit that way before we got into New Age tantra. But he was always willing to try something new—phone sex, cyberporn, bondage, ice cubes. I like men who are adventurous."

"So do I, up to a point. And I haven't been bored once, before or after our marriage."

"All the more reason you should both read *The Holy Sexual Communion* and then join Andrew and me at one of Alida's workshops. You may think you've known sexual intimacy before, but until he learns how to awaken the goddess in you . . ."

Now they were talking as though I'd suddenly disappeared. And not only that, but evaluating my sexual prowess. I'd had enough. I said, "Kerry's goddess is as awake as it's ever going to be and I don't need to feed her dates and nuts or beat on an elkskin drum to keep it awake. I'm going into the kitchen and achieve ultimate intimacy with a cold beer."

"Andrew was stubborn in the beginning too," Paula said serenely. "I'd like another glass of wine while you're out there, if it's not too much trouble."

"I'll get us both another glass," Kerry said before I could answer. A good thing, too, or I might have said something we'd all have regretted.

She followed me out to the kitchen. When the door was shut I said, "Valley of bliss, wand of light . . . Christ. That woman is a card-carrying lunatic."

"Oh, now, Paula's not that bad. And neither is New Age tantra. It's a harmless fad, and I like the basic concept of greater closeness among couples."

"Don't tell me she's got you interested enough to try dragging me to one of her workshops—"

"Of course not. There are better ways to achieve closeness than with silly trappings and euphemisms. I'm not a faddist, sexual or otherwise—you know that."

"Thank God. Sorry if I got a little exercised in there, but Paula pushes my buttons sometimes."

"I know, but you make it worse by provoking her." Kerry opened the refrigerator, handed me a can of Bud. "She's a very needy person. That's why she keeps flitting from one vogue to another. I doubt she'll ever find anything that will make her happy or keep her fulfilled for very long. It's sad, really."

"Yeah. All right, I'll try to cut her some slack. You think Andrew is really into this tantra stuff too?"

"For Paula's sake, I hope so."

For his sake, I thought, I hope not. I watched Kerry refill the two wineglasses from a bottle of Trentadue chardonnay. "You won't let her hang around too long tonight, will you?"

"Just long enough to finish this glass."

"Good. Mind if we don't go out for dinner?"

"No, I wouldn't mind."

"I thought we'd cook something, have a nice, quiet evening alone. I took on a missing persons case today and I've got to go out of town for a few days. Leaving early in the morning."

"Then we'll definitely stay home." She leaned over to kiss me. "If you're good, I'll let you light up my valley later on."

I winced. "Let's just call it making love, okay? And if you ever drag out any scented oils or drums or statues of Buddha, or read just one paragraph aloud from *The Holy Sexual Communion,* I'll divorce you and your goddess both. Grievous mental cruelty."

She grinned and started out. At the door she turned to wink at me. "Don't worry," she said. "I'd never do anything to make you throw a temper tantra."

Temper tantra. Cute. But I couldn't help chuckling after she was gone.

I sat at the table to drink my beer. And while I was sitting there I found myself looking at the refrigerator. I kept on looking at it, frowning a little, listening to Paula's shrill-again voice rise in the living room.

Ice cubes?

4

People who don't live in California, and many who do, have little idea of just how varied the state is, how different one section is from another fifty or five hundred miles away. Geographically and demographically. What sets the northeastern corner—Modoc and Lassen counties—apart from any other region in the state, first, is its remoteness. There are no large or even small cities within a radius of hundreds of miles, no major highways; it takes hours of hard driving through mountainous terrain to get there from San Francisco or Reno or one of the Oregon cities. The area has its share of scenic attractions: Modoc National Forest, South Warner Wilderness Area, Lassen National Forest, dozens of small bodies of water with names like Horse Lake and Moon Lake and Big Sage Reservoir. It also has some of the best hunting and fishing anywhere on the West Coast. But the effort required to get there, and a dearth of the usual tourist amenities, keeps visitors to a minimum even in the summer and fall.

Population is sparse in both counties, Modoc in particular, and a hefty percentage of the Corner's residents prefer it that way. And that is the other thing that sets the Corner apart: the attitudes, beliefs, biases, and overall mind-set of its people. They like their status quo and their privacy; they tolerate hunters, fishermen, skiers, tourists, but unlike the inhabitants of other California rural areas, most don't actively cultivate outsiders. And some of them are insular to the point of clannishness, hostility, even violence.

The largest town up that way is Susanville, population 7,000, in lower Lassen County. Alturas, near the Oregon border in Modoc County, has half as many residents. The rest of the towns in the two counties are either villages or wide spots along highways 395, 299, and 139—places most native Californians have never even heard of, much less visited. Newell, Fort Bidwell, Lake City, Cedarville, Davis Creek, Likely, Madeline, Termo, Ravendale.

And Creekside. Creekside, California, population 112.

I pulled in there at four-thirty on Tuesday afternoon, after nearly six long hours of driving, the last hundred miles over roads still snow-hemmed even though it was well into spring. It wasn't much by anybody's standards. Wide spot just off Highway 395 at the northern border of Lassen County, rimmed by mountains and closely edged on all sides by pine and fir forests. Two-block main drag, winter-potholed, and some short side streets that gave access to an old white hillside church with a high steeple and bell tower and a scattering of houses and newer log cabins squatting among the trees. The business establishments were few and mostly on the east side of Main. Creekside General Store. Trilby's Hardware & Electric, "We Sell Natural Gas." Modoc Cafe. Eagle's Roost Bar and Card Room, "Dancing Every Saturday Nite." Maxe's Service and Garage. And at the far end, near the second of two access roads that took you to and from 395—Northern Comfort Cabins, Off-Season Rates, Vacancy.

I turned into the driveway next to the rustic Northern Comfort sign. The motel was not particularly inviting, even to a weary traveler who had been on the road since eight A.M. A dozen small pineboard cabins set in twin rows of six that faced one another across an unpaved courtyard like old soldiers on a run-down parade ground. The office, which appeared to double as living quarters for the owners, was larger but just as old and not as straight-standing: seedy drill instructor fronting his motley troops. Behind the last of the cabins, where the trees grew in close, a stream ran fast and frothy—the creek, probably, that had given the hamlet its name.

There were no other cars to keep mine company except for an old Buick with its chrome snout peeking out from behind the office, where the owners' living quarters were. The whole place had the look of desertion, even with lights on inside the office and smoke twisting out of a rear chimney. I stepped out into a fast-gathering twilight. Cold up here; you could still taste winter in the air. The rush-and-hiss of the stream running was audible even at a distance of a hundred yards, swollen as it was with snow runoff.

The stream made me think of trout, fat rainbow trout, and the feel of my old fly rod with its Daiwa reel, and the way a mountain creek tugs and swirls around your legs. How long since I'd gotten away for a few days of fishing? Long time. Hell, at least three years. Kerry didn't care for "murdering innocent fish," as she called it. None of my male friends were fishermen, and I couldn't seem to work up enough enthusiasm to go off by myself for the two or three days it would take to get to and then fish a worthwhile trout stream. The last time I'd tied a fly or set a hook for a rainbow had been up in the Sierras, on the Middle Fork south of Quincy. Eberhardt and me, a few months before we'd busted up our friendship and our partnership. Packed in for three days, caught our limit on the first, and spent the rest of the time swilling beer and pretending that we were still as close as we'd once been. . . .

Eberhardt.

The hell with him. And the hell with pointless nostalgia. I didn't need good old Eb and he didn't need me, for trout fishing or any other damn thing. Friendships die natural deaths the same as people do. Why keep poking around among the bones?

I flexed some driving kinks out of my shoulders and back and entered the motel office. Small, rustic, dingy. On one wall was a framed, hand-stitched motto that said *Praise God;* on another was a brass sculpture of a cross and a pair of praying hands. There was nobody behind the narrow counter at the back, not until I bellied up to it. Then a door opened and a tall, cadaverous party came through. He moved in a slow, painful shuffle, as if he had back or leg problems. He was about my age, late fifties, with a beak of a nose and loose skin in folds under his chin and ears and hair that poked up in thin, wispy patches around his scalp. He put me in mind of a molting turkey.

"Help you?"

"I'd like a cabin."

"Sure thing. Just tonight or longer?"

"Probably just tonight."

"Got your pick," he said. "Close to the road or farther back. Cabins in back are real quiet."

"Quiet is what I like."

"Give you number twelve."

He put a key and a registration card on my side of the countertop. I laid a credit card and the photograph of Allison McDowell on his side. As soon as he saw the photo, his face closed up. He looked at it for several seconds, his chin tucked down in its nest of wattles. When his head finally came up, his eyes told me nothing at all.

He said, "Police officer?"

"Private investigator."

"Girl's family?"

"What about her family?"

"They the ones hired you?"

"My client's identity is confidential."

"Well," he said, "I already told the sheriff's man everything I know. Which ain't much."

"Mind telling me too, Mr.—?"

"Bartholomew," grudgingly. "Ed."

"Mr. Bartholomew."

"They checked in, they spent the night, they left next morning. I never even seen him. Girl came in for the room. Otherwise—"

"Otherwise what?"

He shook his head.

"Late afternoon when they checked in, right?" I asked. "Week ago Saturday, about this time."

"That's right."

"Which cabin did you give them?"

"Eleven. In back, opposite the one I give you. But they didn't leave nothing behind. My wife does the cleaning up; she'd of found it if they had."

"What time did they check out on Sunday?"

"Didn't check out. Just left the key in the cabin."

"So Allison paid in advance."

"In advance. Made one call, but she put that on her own phone card."

"Did you see them leave?"

"No," Bartholomew said. "Told you, I never seen the two of 'em together. Or him at all."

"How about your wife?"

"She never seen him either."

"So you can't give me a description of the man."

"No. Ask Art Maxe, down at the garage. He seen him."

"Allison didn't put his name on the registration card?"

"Just hers."

"You didn't ask for it?"

"No reason to. Law says only one name's required."

"She didn't mention it? First name, nickname?"

"Just said her friend. Boyfriend. Some other time I wouldn't of rented to her."

"Why?"

"Why did I? It's slow time and we need the money."

"No, I mean why wouldn't you have rented to her?"

"Wasn't married. No wedding ring. I asked her and she said she wasn't." His lips pursed as if he were tasting something sour. "Sharing a bed out of wedlock is a sin."

"They left Creekside around ten Sunday morning, I understand."

"That's what Art Maxe says. He had their car ready at nine-thirty and they picked it up around then and was gone by ten."

41

"When the girl checked in," I said, "did she happen to mention what route they planned to take from here? Side trips, anything like that?"

"Nosir. All she said was her and her friend been having trouble with their car and they had to have it towed in to Maxe's Garage and wasn't it lucky they was close to a town when it quit on them."

While we'd been talking I had filled out the registration card. As I slid it over to him I said, "Mind if I take number eleven instead of twelve?"

"What for? I told you, nothing in there that'll tell you where them kids went."

"I'd still like eleven. If you don't mind."

"Why should I mind?" he said, and gave me the key to number eleven. I smiled at him before I went out. He didn't smile back.

As with Creekside itself, there wasn't much to the cabin. Small, bare, barely functional—a wooden cell designed for those who came to the Corner expecting to rough it. Four coarse-pine walls, unadorned except for a framed hunting print and, hanging low and off center over the bed, a sepia-toned picture of Christ wearing a crown of thorns. Dresser, nightstand, bedframe, all of scarred pine. New, board-hard mattress covered by a cheap quilt. TV set that had been manufactured about the time of the first Super Bowl. The bathroom was little more than a cubicle with an ancient toilet and a zinc-floored shower. In the old days one of the slang terms for toilet was "growler"; this one reminded me of why. It made noises like an angry Doberman when you flushed it.

Cold in there too. The only heating appliance was a space heater; I switched it on before I sat on the hard mattress. From outside I could hear the muted rush of the stream. It had a lonesome sound.

On the nightstand was a telephone with a little card Scotch-taped to the base that told you all long-distance calls had to go through the office. That figured. I lifted the receiver and buzzed the office, and it was a scratchy-voiced woman who answered—Mrs. Bartholomew, no doubt. I gave her Helen McDowell's private number at In the Mode in Lafayette. She said she'd ring it for me, but she sounded stiff and grudging about it, as if I were asking her to do something that went against her grain.

Helen McDowell answered on the first ring, with the same eager, desperately hopeful tone she'd used on the phone the day before. Which told me before she did that she'd gone through another day of no word from her daughter, no word from Captain Fassbinder. The sound of my name snuffed out the eagerness, flattened the hope again under a dull weariness. Only the desperation remained, poking through the weariness like an object with sharp edges.

"You're in Creekside?" she asked.

"Yes. Just arrived."

"Good." Pause. "This is the first time all day the phone's rung." Pause. "Have you spoken to anyone yet?"

"Just Ed Bartholomew at the motel. I've got a cabin here. He didn't have anything more to tell me than he told you."

"When will you see Art Maxe?"

"He's my next stop. I wanted to check in with you first."

"You'll call me if you find out anything, anything at all?"

"Right away."

"Would you call tomorrow in any case? At this point I need . . ." She didn't finish the sentence.

"I know," I said. "I'll call tomorrow."

"Here at the shop, before five?"

"Before five."

We said quick, hushed good-byes, like furtive lovers, and I rang off feeling vaguely depressed. In my mind was an image of her—the naked hope in her face, the pain and the too-tight control. I got up and went into the bathroom and washed my face and hands in icy tap water. That did nothing for the low feeling. Neither did a couple of turns around the cold, bare room that Allison had shared with her lover ten nights earlier.

Assume the boyfriend was a college student too, someone of her own approximate age. How would they have felt, spending the night in a place like this? Viewed it as part of a brief adventure, maybe—or the beginning of a long shared one. Backwoods interlude; snuggle up in this monastic cell, make love and their own heat, make the best of a minor hitch in their plans. Or maybe it hadn't been that innocent or pleasant. Maybe they'd had a fight of some kind, and the next day it had kindled even hotter, and then . . . what? He abandoned her somewhere in the wilderness, and took her car and drove himself back to Eugene? Not likely, but possible—yet another possibility. Hell, at this stage, with the limited number of facts I had to work with, anything was possible. The car broke down again and this time they weren't lucky enough to be close to a town and they'd managed to get themselves lost on foot. Or they'd had an off-highway accident, in some remote area. Or, as Tamara Corbin had suggested, they'd made the foolish mistake of picking up the kind of hitchhiker who turns out to be deadly. Or—another worst-case scenario, and also as Tamara had suggested—her mystery lover hadn't been what he'd seemed to Allison, was a psycho in sheep's clothing.

Circumstances. Allison's actions plus those of the boyfriend plus those of strangers—piling up, intermingling, creating new circumstances that affected and reshaped their two lives and maybe those of others as well. But what action, what cause and effect? The key was finding just one of the circumstances; then it would be possible to piece together the others, extrapolate, work out the gist of what had happened.

Sure. Except that it had been nine days now, and there hadn't been a whisper from or about them. Not a whisper. And nine days is more than long enough for any trail to grow cold, for events to lose their detail, become distorted, become lost.

The image of Helen McDowell's face flickered across my

mind again, accompanied by the sound of her voice on the phone just now, the desperation in it, the gathering dread. She knew what I knew, what anyone in a situation like this knows. Some refuse to face it, but she wasn't one of those; denial was not in her makeup. And because it wasn't, because she was a woman who met a crisis head-on, each passing, waiting minute would eat at her like drops of acid.

The longer her daughter remained missing without a trace or a whisper, the slimmer the chance of anyone finding any of the right circumstances—of finding her alive, or ever finding her at all.

5

Maxe's Garage was a big, barnlike building made of warped pine boards and covered with a sloping tin roof. A row of three gas pumps, protected from rain and snow by a rickety-looking portico, guarded the narrow apron in front. A couple of pickups, a tow truck, and eight or nine junk cars were scattered along the sides and around to the rear. With its run-down appearance and its dark, colorless aspect, it reminded me of a set in a forties film noir—*Out of the Past,* specifically, except that the kid manning the pumps was blond instead of dark-haired, and judging from the portable radio pumping forth country music from his shirt pocket, not yet deaf.

The kid told me I could find Art Maxe inside the garage. The interior was cluttered, droplit, and had a cement floor so smeared with grease and grit, it appeared to have been painted black. The only occupant had his head and upper body underneath the raised hood of a Brahma four-by-four, working the accelerator linkage to race the engine. I walked up alongside and waited until he quit jazzing the linkage.

"Art Maxe?"

He said, "Yeah?" without shifting position.

I told him who I was and why I was there. That brought him out of the Brahma's shell. He was big and shaggy and dirty, like a bear that had been rolling around in a pile of oily refuse. There were oil streaks on his unshaven cheeks, a glob of grease caught in his unkempt black hair; his overalls might never have been washed and his hands were black-spotted with the kind of embedded grime even industrial-strength soap never quite gets out. He gave me a long, steady look out of squinty eyes that held both wariness and suspicion.

"I already talked to the county cops," he said.

"Then you won't mind talking to me. I'm trying to do the same job—find a couple of missing kids."

He shrugged. "You ask me, those two took a side road somewheres and that crappy MG of theirs busted down again. Lot of wilderness around here, lot of places to get lost."

"Her MG really that bad?"

"Piece of junk. Just about ready for the dismantlers."

"What made it quit running out on the highway?"

"Fuel pump went out. I didn't have one in stock, not for a foreign job like that; had to call down to Susanville. They couldn't get it up here until late Saturday. Special trip."

"You had the car ready for them at ten Sunday morning?"

"That's right," Maxe said. "Told the girl it'd cost her extra, my working on Sunday, but she said that was all right, they wanted to get back on the road. I warned 'em, though, both of 'em. Half a dozen other things ready to go wrong on that baby. Don't push it too hard, I said. She just laughed. Allison, right?"

"Allison McDowell."

"Kids that age, everything's a big joke."

"Did she pay you, or was it the boyfriend?"

"She did. Cash. I give her a little off the bill for cash."

"Who was driving when they left?"

"She was."

"They say which direction they were heading?"

"Not to me. Out to the highway and then who knows?"

"How did they seem together that morning?"

"Seem?"

"Toward each other. Were they getting along all right?"

"Better than all right," Maxe said. "Just like the day before—kidding around, laughing, holding hands. Christ, even kissing on each other." He shook his head and made a spitting mouth, as if he thought public displays of affection were in poor taste.

"Either of them mention his name?" I asked.

"Not that I remember."

"First name, even a pet name?"

"I didn't pay that much attention."

"How old would you say he was?"

"Her age, about."

"Describe him."

"Shit, I'm no good at that. . . ."

"Didn't the county law ask you for a description?"

Shrug. "I told that sheriff's captain, Fassbinder, what I could remember. Wasn't much."

"How tall was he? The boyfriend."

"Not too tall. Average."

"Six feet? Shorter?"

"Six feet, I guess."

"Weight?"

"One-seventy, one-eighty."

"In good shape?"

"Well, he filled out a sweater pretty good."

"What about his hair? Long, short?"

"Short. Real short."

"What color?"

"Well, what color you think?"

"I'm asking you, Mr. Maxe."

"Black."

"Any memorable feature? Mouth, eyes, nose?"

"No."

"Scars, moles?"

"No."

"Anything at all unusual about him?"

". . . I dunno what you mean."

"Did he limp, talk oddly—like that?"

"No. He was just a . . . just a kid, that's all."

"How was he dressed?"

"Blue sweater, Levis, them running shoes."

"Both days?"

"Yeah."

"And the girl?"

"Same, only her sweater was green."

"Was anybody else here when they came on Sunday morning? Anybody they might've talked to?"

"No."

"Kid out on the pumps?"

"No, just me. Johnny don't work on Sundays." Maxe made a waggly gesture with the wrench he was holding. "I got work to do," he said. "How about you letting me get back to it, huh?"

"Okay."

"Questions like you been asking ain't gonna find 'em anyway. They got lost somewheres, like I said. Walk out under their own steam or the sheriff's pilots'll find 'em from the air. Otherwise . . ." Another shrug. "Bones," he said.

There were two people in the Creekside General Store when I walked in: behind the counter, a heavyset woman in a plaid lumberman's shirt, and in front of it, a bushy-bearded male customer wearing a stocking cap over long, graying hair tied in a ponytail. It was a dark, crowded place, almost as dark as Maxe's Garage, with a creosote-soaked wood floor, narrow aisles, and tall shelves. In addition to the usual merchandise, it sported a back section stocked with old clothing and miscellany, a sign above it reading THRIFT CORNER.

I loitered near the door, waiting for the counter transaction to be finished. On the wall was a corkboard to which were attached dozens of business cards, flyers, scraps of notepaper with handwriting on them. People wanting goods and services; people selling same. Cordwood, yard work and hauling, and baby-sitting were the dominant subjects.

One of the flyers was something else again—something ugly. It had been printed by an outfit called the Christian National Emancipation League, run by a "grand pastor" named Richard Artemus Chaffee—one of those white supremacist outfits that preach hate instead of love under the guise of religion. It wasn't local; the address and telephone number were downstate in Modesto. Put here by a traveling league member, probably: recruitment drive that reached even into backwaters like this one. I quit reading it when the stocking-capped customer came away from the counter with his purchases. But I would have quit anyway about then. Credos such as "dedicated to purifying America of race-mixing and mongrelism, and to the emancipation of the white seed and the rise and rebirth of God's true Chosen People" make me want to puke.

The ponytailed guy was pushing fifty, and the length of his hair and beard, the out-of-date ragbag clothing he wore, marked him as a child of the sixties—an unreconstructed hippie for whom time had stopped somewhere around 1967. He didn't want anything to do with me, maybe because to him I represented the establishment in my conservative suit and tie. He shook his head when I tried to talk to him, refused to look at Allison McDowell's photograph, and pushed past me and out through the door. Peace and love to you too, brother, I thought.

The heavyset woman was even less cooperative. She glowered at me as I approached, said before I got to her, "Don't bother showing it to me neither. I can't help you."

"I just want to know—"

"I know what you want to know. I never saw those two kids, neither one."

"At least take a look at the girl's photo—"

"Can't help you, mister. Didn't you hear me tell you that? This is a store, not an information booth. Buy something or leave."

I left. On the way out I tore down the Christian National

Emancipation League's flyer and crumpled it and tossed it into a sidewalk trash can. That made me feel a little better.

Trilby's Hardware & Electric was closed, so I moved on to the Modoc Cafe. Too-hot box, its trapped air thick and miasmic with the odors of frying meat, grease, coffee, cigarettes, and various human effluvium. Booths along the side walls, a few tables in the middle, serving counter and kitchen at the rear. The patrons totaled six, all in the left-hand booths; it was early yet, not much past five-thirty. I sat in one of the right-hand booths and waited for the lone waitress to work her way around to me.

She was fortyish, tired, with a polite outer layer over a hard inner core of cynicism and quiet desperation: it went with the job in places like this, or maybe it was the job that made women like her the way they were. Her name was Lena, according to one of those little oblong name tags on the pocket of her uniform. She set a well-thumbed menu in front of me, asked if I wanted coffee.

I said I did and then held up Allison's photo. She glanced at it, took a longer look at me. The cynicism was plain in her eyes now, along with a guardedness, but none of the polite veneer seemed to have chipped away. Even her faint professional smile remained intact.

She said, "And who would you be?"

"Private investigator."

"No kidding." She wasn't impressed, or even particularly interested—at least not in me or my origins.

"You recognize the girl?"

"If you mean was she in here, yeah, she was. Only place to eat in town."

"Week ago Saturday night?"

"As I remember."

"With a male companion?"

"Him too."

"You wait on them?"

"I'm the only waitress when I'm here."

"Did she happen to mention her friend's name?"

"Once that I heard. It was noisy, so I'm not sure if I heard it right."

"What name do you think you heard?"

"Rob."

"Rob, not Bob?"

"Rob."

"Anything about him strike you as unusual?"

"Not really. Good-looking kid, not too dark."

"What ethnic background, would you say?"

Her smile dipped wryly. "I wouldn't."

"Did he have an accent? I mean regional, not foreign."

"Not so's I noticed."

"How did the two of them act together?"

"Like they were alone in a bedroom."

"Couldn't keep their hands off each other?"

"Not for two seconds. In a place like this, in the middle of the Saturday dinner rush . . . stupid. Very stupid."

"Why stupid?"

"Calling attention to themselves like that."

"Yes?"

"These're the mountains, mister, not the big city." Lena poked a stray lock of brown hair back over one ear. "Coffee, you said. Cream, sugar?"

"Just black."

She went away and I opened the menu. I hadn't eaten since breakfast, and then only juice and a bowl of Grape Nuts with Kerry, and I was pretty hungry. The closest thing to low-fat, low-cholesterol food served here was pot roast, and I was not in the mood for pot roast, particularly not when I saw the listing for chicken-fried steak with country gravy.

I have had a small insatiable lust for chicken-fried steak all my adult life. Back in the days when I was forty pounds overweight and shoveling in all the wrong things, I would order it every time I saw it on a menu—ongoing search for the ultimate chicken-fried steak, blue-collar equivalent of the white-collar pursuit for a perfect martini. I have kept my weight down for well over four years now, after shedding the extra forty pounds under the grimmest circumstances imaginable; retrained myself to eat and drink in healthy moderation, and to maintain a more or less regular exercise program. I hadn't had chicken-fried steak in all that time and I was overdue. One little indulgence wouldn't hurt me. One little rationalization, either.

Lena came back with my coffee and I ordered the chicken-fried steak. Then I asked her, "Allison and Rob have much to say to you while they were here?"

"No. Too wrapped up in each other for chitchat."

"Just placed their orders and that was all?"

"Pretty much."

"What were they talking to each other about?"

"I didn't pay much attention."

"Travel plans? Anything along those lines?"

"I just told you, I didn't pay much attention."

"Did they talk to anyone else, one of the other customers?"

". . . No."

"Why the hesitation?"

Lena looked down at her pad, moving her lips in an over-and-under fashion as if she were holding a debate with herself. Pretty soon she said, "Not in here. Afterward, out front."

"Who'd they talk to then?"

"I don't know. I saw them through the window, just for a few seconds, and it was steamy in here and dark outside."

"One person or more?"

"Two. Two men, I think."

"But you don't have any idea who they were?"

"Think I'm lying about that?"

"No, I don't think you're lying. How long did the conversation go on?"

"Couldn't have been long," Lena said. "Next time I glanced through the window, they were gone. All of them."

"What time was that, do you remember?"

"End of the dinner rush . . . about seven-thirty."

"You see the kids again that night?"

"No."

"Sunday morning, before they left town?"

"I wasn't here. I don't work Sundays."

"Who does?"

"Breakfast shift? Lorraine. Ask her tomorrow morning."

"I'll do that. Thanks."

"Mashed potatoes or french fries with your steak?"

"Mashed potatoes."

Her mouth quirked again. "Good choice," she said.

It wasn't. Turned out I'd made a lousy choice all around. The mashed potatoes managed to be lumpy and runny at the same time, and more than likely had come out of a box; the country gravy was mostly white sauce with neither Tabasco nor black pepper; and the patty-sized "steak" was a mass of gristle coated with corn meal instead of flour. If the perfect chicken-fried steak was a ten, this one barely made it past zero. No wonder Lena's smile had been wry.

So the ultimate chicken-fried steak was still out there somewhere. Maybe. Or maybe, like the putative perfect martini—or for that matter, like Diogenes' genuinely honest man—it didn't really exist except as an illusionary ideal. Not that it mattered either way. The important thing was the quest itself, the search for perfection in an imperfect world.

6

The Eagle's Roost was like every back-country tavern I'd ever set foot in, down to the heads and horns of dead animals displayed on the walls and the jukebox packed with sob-and-throb country tunes. At one end was a tiny dance floor and bandstand, and beyond that, through an archway, was the card room. Both the bar and the card room were moderately crowded, to the point where nobody paid much attention to me. Walk into an unfamiliar watering hole like this when only a few regulars were present and they'd all stop what they were doing to give you the once-over, wonder who you were and why you'd wandered onto their turf. Walk into a place like this when it was crowded and the opposite happened: you weren't an individual, just another cell in the crowd body. That was the way it was with lynch mobs too. And one of the reasons strangers can incite men who would not even speak to them under other circumstances.

I made my way to the only empty stool at the bar, at the far end. There were two bartenders and the one working this end was rail-thin, about as jolly as a slug on a dry rock and just as slow; it took him nearly five minutes to get around to where I was sitting. I used the time to flash Allison's photo at the rough-dressed men on either side of me. None of them wanted anything to do with it or with a reasonably well-attired stranger; I was interrupting their happy hour and their penetrating discussions about deer hunting, baseball, and whether or not dynamite was the best method of uprooting a stubborn tree stump.

One, a fat, balding guy wearing suspenders went so far as to give me a dirty look, climb off his stool, and clump away into the men's room.

When the meatless bartender finally acknowledged my presence, I tried the photo on him. His interest was likewise nil. He said with annoyance, "Can't you see I'm busy?"

"Just take a look," I said. "It's the girl who disappeared last week—"

"I don't know anything about that."

"I didn't say you did. I'm only trying—"

"You drinking or what?"

"Not right now."

"Then don't take up that stool, huh?"

He moved away, and I thought: Bad idea, trying to work cooperation out of a bunch of backwoods Bud-suckers. Let it go for now. Come back later, maybe, when it's not so crowded. Or, hell, why bother? Even if any of the Eagle's Roost patrons knew anything, they weren't likely to tell me about it, drunk or sober.

I slid off the stool, got one foot down on the floor—and somebody bumped me from behind, hard enough to put me into a lurch and stagger. I caught myself in time to avoid slamming into a woman heading for the bar. When I straightened and came around, I was looking at the fat, balding guy who'd given me the dirty look.

"Whyn't you watch where you're going?" he said with his lips peeled back. Dog-snarl look, dog-snarl voice.

Looking for trouble, I thought. I could see it in his jowly face, his little pig eyes. Why? One of those belligerent types who turn mean when they drink, maybe. Or maybe he just didn't like strangers asking questions and showing photographs of missing kids.

Trouble was something I didn't need, not in a place like this. I said, keeping my voice even, "Sorry. Guess I didn't see you."

"Yeah? Next time pay attention. Otherwise you'll wind up bouncing on your ass."

Anything I said would only provoke him; I stayed silent. Some of the drinkers at the bar were swung around on their stools, watching us.

The fat guy came ahead and poked my chest with a hard, blunt forefinger. "Whyn't you go back where you come from?"

I kept my hands down at my sides and my mouth shut. But my eyes held his in a flat, unblinking stare. I wanted him to know that I wasn't afraid of him, that I felt the same dislike for him he felt for me.

He moved even closer, tried to prod me with his bulging paunch. I wouldn't prod; my feet were set apart and all my weight was bunched forward. Big as he was, he would've had better luck trying to move a wall.

"Leave him alone, Frank," somebody at the bar said. "What the hell?"

The fat guy ignored that. He said to me, right up in my face, "You ain't wanted in Creekside. Get me?"

"I get you." I smelled him too; his breath stank of beer and cigarettes and a bad case of pyorrhea. Enough of this crap, I thought. I said, "Okay, Frank. Back off now."

"Suppose I don't, asshole?"

"Then one of two things will happen. Either we'll stand here like this all night, nose to nose, or you'll have to try prodding me some more. If you prod me, one of two things will happen."

"Yeah?"

"Yeah. I'll resist enough to make you take a swing at me and then I'll go file an assault charge with the county law. Or I'll just plain resist and then we'll get into it good and you'll be the one who winds up bouncing on his ass."

One of the stool-sitters snickered. I wasn't the only one in there who didn't like fatso's mean-dog act.

"What's it going to be?" I said. "Your choice."

"Tough one, eh, Frank?" somebody else said, and there were more snickers.

The fat guy was used to being the aggressor; I'd put him on the defensive and that was a role he didn't know how to handle. Being laughed at by his friends—if he had any—and his neighbors unsettled him too. For about thirty seconds nothing happened and it could have gone either way. Then, jerkily, he glanced around, didn't find much support in the watching faces, and I saw his shoulders sag a little and I knew I'd backed him down.

He knew it too. He said lamely, "Screw this, you ain't worth the hassle," and backed up a pace, glaring. After a few seconds he turned and hoisted his lard onto his stool.

It had gotten quiet in there, but now that the floor show was over, the noise started again: loud voices and plenty of laughter. I made my way toward the door, not hurrying. I was two-thirds of the way there when somebody at one of the tables reached up to flick at my coat sleeve. My first thought was that it was more trouble, and I came around fast and tense; I was in no mood for a repeat performance.

But it wasn't more trouble. The sleeve-plucker was Art Maxe, slouched in a chair with a bottle of Bud (what else?) in one hand and a cancer stick in the other, grinning up at me. Across from him sat a tall scarecrow of a man with dirty-blond hair, bright eyes, cratered cheeks. The scarecrow seemed to think I was worth gawking at. He wasn't quite smiling, but I had the impression there was laughter lurking somewhere inside him.

Maxe said, "Handled yourself pretty good over there. Think you could've taken him in a fight?"

"What do you think?"

"I bet Ollie here ten that you could. Frank's a tub of hot air." He sucked in smoke, let it dribble out slowly before he spoke again. "Dunno why you're bothering to show that girl's picture around. Kids got lost somewhere, like I told you."

"I get paid to bother."

"Tell me something? I always wondered."

"What's that?"

"Your business—you make good bread?"

"I make a living."

"Just a living? Must not be very good at it."

"I usually get results."

"In the city. Not up here."

"No?"

"These mountains, they got secrets no outsider can find out. Some we can't even find out ourselves."

The laughter quit lurking inside the skinny guy and came out in a thin, high-pitched giggle. I didn't like hearing it; it made me think of Richard Widmark in *Kiss of Death,* just before he shoved the old lady in the wheelchair down the stairs.

"What's funny?" I asked him.

"Nothin'," he said. "Nothin's funny."

"You wouldn't have anything to tell about the missing kids, would you?"

"Who, me? Not me, man. I don't know nothing about nothing—do I, Art?"

"Not unless it has to do with beer, dogs, or pussy," Maxe said.

"Yeah, and I drink so much of the first, sometimes I get the last two mixed up."

Bad old joke between them; they whooped it up together, the scarecrow slapping the table hard enough to make the bottles and glasses on it dance a little jig. Maxe rescued his Bud before it tipped over and then winked at me. "Don't mind Ollie," he said. He tapped his temple. "Everybody around here says old Ollie Ballard ain't all there and I guess they're right. How about it, Ollie? You playing with a full deck or not?"

"Couple of aces missing," Ballard said, "but the joker's still there. Yessir, the *joker's* still there."

His shrill giggle followed me out, lingered in my ears like a slow-dying echo even after I shut the door. Couple of aces missing, all right. His laughter was the kind you'd hear in an asylum around three A.M.

As early as it was—not even seven o'clock—Main Street and the side streets were empty of cars and pedestrians. No night life here; just the tavern and the cafe and the comforts of home and hearth, such as they might be. I buttoned my topcoat and turned north along the cracked sidewalk. The Northern Comfort Cabins were only a little more than a block away, close enough so that I'd walked down earlier rather than bother with the car.

The noise from the Eagle's Roost faded as I moved away from the entrance; silence settled in around me. Darkness too: there was no moon, Creekside was too small to have streetlamps, and the wide-spaced house and building lights shone hard, brittle, without much warmth and without penetrating the night's hard black shell. The air was sharp-cold, stirred by a high wind running clouds down the sky; it felt thin in my lungs, heavy in my nostrils with the rich scent of pine and fir. Crisp, early-spring mountain night—the kind made for a brisk walk, the kind that ought to lift your spirits. Not mine, though. Not in Creekside, California, population 112.

I didn't much care for this little pimple on the backside of nowhere. In fact, I was beginning to detest it. Maybe it was because I was an intruder and had been made to feel like one at every turn. Maybe it was the people I'd encountered during the brief time I'd been there—Bartholomew, Maxe, the aging hippie and the woman in the general store, Ollie Ballard, the thin, snotty bartender, and the fat blowhard named Frank. Maybe it was the lousy chicken-fried steak. Or maybe there wasn't any specific reason, just the fact that some places, regardless of size or location, generate negative energy that affects certain people. Different places for different individuals. Anyone who is at all sensitive to his surroundings has experienced this at least once, a distaste and an unease that you can't seem to shake while you're there.

I crossed an unpaved side street, stubbing my toe halfway along on a dark-hidden jut of rock. Yeah, right: even the inanimate parts of Creekside didn't want me around. I laughed a little to myself, or at myself, and went on toward the pale, cold spotlight that illuminated the Northern Comfort sign. There was no sidewalk on this block of Main, and the downsloping verge was muddy and held the faint black shine of water; I had to walk out on the road. Not far onto the asphalt—I was no more than two paces from its edge.

The first awareness I had of the car coming behind me was the growl of its engine as the driver downshifted to a lower gear. It sounded close, but not close enough to alarm me or make me turn my head. For a few more seconds I walked in darkness; then light from a pair of headlamps splashed around and ahead of me, creating a goblinlike elongation of my shadow. There was another growling downshift, gears grinding this time, and in the next second a sudden blare of sound—an air horn as loud as a truck's—that caused me to jerk and pivot at the same time.

The headlights seemed to be rushing straight at me, huge and blinding in the darkness. They slewed away to the left just as I flung myself opposite to the right. Brakes and tires squealed. Somebody yelled something profane. I landed on my right foot, my body twisted sideways, and the foot slipped and slid in the mud; I lost my balance and went down hard on my tailbone, slid some more on one hip before I could get my hands down to act as brakes. But it wasn't until my feet sliced ankle-deep through chill water, then jarred against the bottom of the ditch, that the slide finally ended.

I was shaken but not really hurt. And mad as hell. I hauled around, wincing at the shoots of pain in my butt, and scrambled out of the ditch on hands and knees. The car wasn't a car, I saw then, but an open, military-style Jeep; it was stopped at an angle in the middle of the road, its engine muttering and rumbling, the high-beam lights turning a tree-ringed abandoned building on the far side into a yellow-white diorama. Two man-shapes sat in the Jeep, swung around my way but not moving, not making any effort to come to my aid.

That made me even madder. I got my legs under me, walked in a hard, soggy stride to the Jeep. "What the hell's the idea?" I said in the same kind of dog-snarl Frank had used in the tavern. "You almost ran me down!"

Neither of the men said anything in response. Just kept on staring at me. In the faint glow from the dash lights I could tell that the driver was young, early twenties, and that the passenger was at least twice and maybe three times his age. Both wore what looked to be camouflage fatigue outfits, the kind that soldiers and some woodsmen wear; the driver also had a fatigue cap on, turned around so that its bill poked out behind his head. Father and son? I'd never seen either of them before. Nor the Jeep, which had a camouflage paint job to match their outfits.

"You were walking on the road." That came from the older man in a flat, raspy voice that sounded as though it was used to giving orders. His short-bristled head turned slightly into profile as he spoke; he was bull-necked, craggy-jawed, with a nose as long and hooked as a hawk's beak.

"On the *side* of the road," I said. "I couldn't walk in the ditch, could I?"

The driver said without a hint of apology, "I didn't see you right away. Pretty dark along here. And you're wearing dark clothes."

"All right. But you were going too goddamn fast."

"Are you hurt?" the older one asked. Not as if he cared much.

"No, but I could've been."

"We didn't come that close to hitting you."

"That's what you say. I say you were—"

Abruptly he swiveled away from me, facing front. "We're late enough as it is, Ramsey," he said to the driver.

The young one put the transmission in gear. I said, "Hey, wait a minute—" but that was as far as I got before he popped the clutch. The Jeep bucked away, yawing for twenty yards or so until he got it straightened out again, leaving a trail of burned rubber. By the time they passed the Northern Comfort, he was doing at least fifty.

I stood there, still hot, and watched the Jeep's taillights grow smaller and then disappear around a turn, out toward the highway. Crazy bastards, driving like that through town. No matter what the older one had said, they'd come pretty damn close to running me down—

A thought crawled into my head: Yeah, they had. And what if they'd done it on purpose? Some kind of warning to quit snooping around on their turf?

No, that was paranoid thinking. Nobody I'd talked to had seemed particularly worried about my presence, or about my finding out anything incriminating; everyone's main interest seemed to be in my going away and leaving them alone. So why should a couple of strangers want to stir me up when it was obvious to anyone with half a brain that I'd be leaving soon anyway? The incident was just what it seemed: a near accident, brought about by carelessness and compounded by disregard for the rights and feelings of anybody but the two rednecks in the Jeep.

I'll be glad to leave in the morning, all right, I thought as I trudged wet and cold and frustrated to the motel. The earlier the better.

7

Wednesday was a bust.

I checked out of the Northern Comfort at eight A.M. There were streaks of dried mud on my topcoat that I hadn't been able to clean off; and my shoes, the only pair I had with me, were badly scuffed and still damp, even though I'd laid them out in front of the cabin's space heater overnight. I'd be lucky if I didn't develop a head cold as another memento of my visit to Creekside.

From the motel I drove down to the Modoc Cafe. Not for breakfast—the eggs would probably contain salmonella and Christ knew what the coffee would do to my digestive tract—but to find out if Lorraine, the early-shift waitress, had anything to tell me about Allison and her friend, Rob. She hadn't. She possessed the same inner core of cynicism and quiet desperation as Lena, but none of the pleasant veneer; she answered my questions with scowls and monosyllables, the gist of her responses being that the missing kids hadn't stopped for food or coffee or anything else on their way out of town. I'd expected as much. They had no doubt wanted shut of Creekside as badly as I did.

I felt better when I was out on Highway 395, heading south. The weather, at least, was cooperating. Mist lay among the trees at the higher elevations, and there was a sheen of wetness on the road, but the sun was out and the clouds of the night before had all blown inland. The sky had that bright, ceramic-blue quality you usually see on clear mornings after a heavy rain.

There was a string of hamlets between Creekside and Susanville; I stopped in each of them, showed Allison's photo and asked my questions in cafes and grocery stores, at service stations. Covering the same ground as Captain Fassbinder, no doubt, and getting the same head shakes and blank stares. I was treated to more of the same at three gas stations, a Denny's, and a Lyon's on the outskirts of the Lassen county seat.

My first stop in the town itself was at a shopping center, where I spent eighty bucks in a shoe store to put some dry leather on my feet. Eighty bucks that I couldn't in all good conscience charge to Helen McDowell on the expense account. Then I found my way to the Sheriff's Department, where I spent an unproductive fifteen minutes with Ralph Fassbinder. He was a lean, energetic type in his late forties, with no apparent bias against private detectives; he treated me cordially enough, but he also wasn't very forthcoming or encouraging.

"Still no leads," he said, "not even the hint of one. No ID on the McDowell girl's boyfriend yet, either."

"His first name might be Rob."

"Oh? Where'd you pick that up?"

"Modoc Cafe in Creekside. Waitress named Lena."

"I talked to her. She didn't mention it to me."

I shrugged. Either she had a natural aversion to county cops or he hadn't asked her the right questions.

"Anyway," Fassbinder said, "we need more than a first name and a general description to ID him. Besides, it may not mean anything when we do—in terms of the disappearance, I mean."

"You don't think they disappeared in Lassen County, do you?"

"Frankly, I don't. It could've happened in a dozen others between here and the Bay Area."

"I know it."

"Pretty big haystack."

"And we're just two guys with pitchforks."

"You said it. Two guys with pitchforks, and too damn much hay, and in my case, too many other chores to do."

"One of us could get lucky."

"I wouldn't count on it," he said.

I ate a sandwich I didn't really want at a deli downtown. After which I used one of the restaurant's pay phones to make a couple of credit-card calls. The first was to my office to check in with Tamara. About the only thing of interest she had to tell me was that Barney Rivera had called again that morning.

"He tell you what he wanted this time?"

"Personal, the man said. Did say it has to do with a mutual friend."

"Mutual friend. But not which one?"

"Nope. I asked but he wouldn't say."

"So he'll call again?"

"Wants you to call him."

"Well, he can wait. What I'm doing up here is a hell of a lot more important than Barney Rivera."

"You have any luck in Creekside?"

"Not much. Place turned out to be a pain in the ass—literally."

"Say again?"

"Never mind. I'll fill you in when I get back."

The second call was to In the Mode in Lafayette. To report my one slim piece of news—that Allison's lover's name might be Rob—to Helen McDowell. The name didn't mean anything to her. She was sure, she said, that her daughter had never mentioned a Rob in connection with the university or Eugene or in any other context.

I told her I would spend the rest of the day canvassing the area, but that if I didn't turn up anything to keep me in the Corner, I would try another tack—drive to Eugene, see if I could ID Rob, and if I could, talk to people who knew him. I didn't tell her I wanted to identify and find out more about the man because he might be the cause of Allison's disappearance rather than a victim himself. But at some level she must have known it anyway; the possibility of foul play had surely occurred to her, even though we'd both been careful not to mention it during any of our conversations. It was to her credit that she didn't question me, as some clients did. She'd hired me to do a job, and what counted for her was that I was doing it.

From Susanville I drove another twenty miles south on 395, stopping in Janesville, Buntingville, and Milford and showing Allison's photo to gas jockeys, waitresses, store clerks. Zero recognition. It was midafternoon when I finished in Milford. No point in continuing any farther south, not with a lot of miles left to travel that day and another long, tedious drive ahead of me the next.

Back up 395 instead, through Susanville, through the mountains and past Creekside and on into Alturas—better than a hundred miles of high-desert and wilderness twists and turns that left me weary and rump-sprung. The only AAA-rated motels in all of Modoc County were in Alturas, testimony to how small and mountainous and sparsely settled the county is, and I was fortunate that the best of them had a vacancy. The single room I was given was palatial compared to cabin eleven at the Northern Comfort. It had central heating, a shower that worked without complaint and provided plenty of hot water, and a direct-dial phone—all the amenities of home.

After dinner I called Kerry to let her know I was still alive and kicking. She said she was glad to hear my voice, but she sounded harried and a little on the grumpy side. "You caught me in the middle of a mess. It's been an infuriating day."

"Paula hasn't been bugging you with more of that tantra nonsense, has she?"

"No, no, it's not Paula. It's a new account I got stuck with yesterday—Luau Shirts of Honolulu. The owner is driving me crazy."

"How come?"

"Because he's an idiot."

"That bad?"

"Worse. A *monumental* idiot named Arthur Dykstra."

"What's the matter with him?"

"He's one of those people who become successful in spite of

themselves," Kerry said. "Started on a shoestring five years ago and now he's the biggest manufacturer of men's and women's Hawaiian shirts in the islands. Not the cheap variety; the fancy art deco aloha type made out of silk crepe de chine that cost a hundred and fifty dollars apiece. Now he's expanding his operations to the mainland, starting in northern California—that's why he hired us."

"Sounds like a relatively easy sell to me."

"It would be if it weren't for the slogan he's come up with for his ads. I can't talk him out of it, and if I have to use it, the whole campaign will be a failure and a joke and I'll be the one to get the blame."

"What kind of slogan could be that terrible?"

" 'Shirt Happens,' " she said.

I burst out laughing.

"It's not funny. My God, can you believe the man is serious? A pun based on a scatological bumper sticker to sell fancy Hawaiian shirts to families. Dykstra thinks people will find it 'amusing' and 'charming.' I've told him over and over how wrong he is, Doug Bates has told him, but he just won't listen. The man is just an *idiot*. . . ."

I let her rant. She seemed to need a sympathetic ear, and I did not feel much like talking about my busted Wednesday or my experiences in Creekside the night before. And just hearing Kerry's voice lifted my spirits—the old tonic working its usual miracle cure.

By God, I loved that woman. I loved her more than I could ever put into words, to her or even to myself.

I was on the road again at eight on Thursday morning. Highway 299 east from Alturas to Canby, then 139 north into Oregon—and except for an occasional logging truck and pokey camper, I had the northbound sides of both highways pretty much to myself. I stopped in Klamath Falls for gas and food and then deadheaded straight through to Eugene, a push of a little more than three hours.

The weather up there wasn't half as pleasant as it had been in the Corner. Oregon is a wet state—the University of Oregon's sports teams are not known as the Ducks for frivolous reasons—and wet was what I encountered: drizzles above Roseburg, steadily increasing rain as I rolled northward. By the time I reached the city I was in the midst of a downpour.

Like a lot of Oregon, Eugene is a green place. That's your first impression and the one that lingers after you've gone away. The city lies between the foothills of the Cascade and Coast mountain ranges, and along the Willamette River—the center of a rich agricultural and lumbering region. I'd spent some time there on a case years back; it had struck me then as a nice town to live in despite the weather. Nothing about it had changed to alter that impression as I drove through it now.

The house Allison McDowell shared with the other U of O students was on Hilyard just off 22nd, within walking distance of the campus. Neighborhood of older homes, built in the twenties and thirties, many of them now converted into off-campus student housing. Wraparound front porch on Allison's, gingerbread still clinging tenaciously to its balustrades and dormers. There were no cars in front or in the driveway, but I parked and tried the bell anyway. Nobody home.

It was a short drive from Hilyard to the city center. The Unicorn Bookstore, where Allison worked part-time, was on Willamette. I had to leave my car a block and a half away and I was moist when I walked in. Big place, new and used stock of both textbooks and general trade books; packed with students and fussy-looking, untidily dressed older persons who might have been teachers or bookish retirees or, hell, homeless people seeking knowledge as well as shelter on a rainy day. The store's manager was in his early twenties, bespectacled and so chinless, it looked as though a bite had been taken out of the lower half of his face. His name was Peverell.

Helen McDowell had talked to him, too, on the phone, so he

knew the situation. He seemed concerned and sympathetic, if a little fussy and much older than his years, like one of his senior customers in training. "I can't understand it," he said. "Allison is such a responsible person."

"I'm sure she is. When she asked for a few days off, what did she tell you?"

"That she needed the time for a trip home to see her mother. It was short notice, but that was Easter break week and we try to be flexible."

"She didn't give any particular reason for the trip?"

"No," Peverell said. "But it seemed important to her. She was . . . excited about it."

"Did you have any idea she was making the trip with a male friend?"

"Not until her mother told me."

"His name may be Rob."

"Rob. Well."

"Know anybody by that name?"

"I don't think so. No, I'm sure I don't."

"Did Allison mention a new man in her life? Any reference along those lines?"

"No, she didn't. She isn't one to talk about personal things."

"Do you know any of her male friends?"

"Well . . . just Gary Oster."

"And he is?"

Peverell shrugged. "A fellow she was seeing."

"Recently?"

"Yes."

"Casual or serious?"

"Casual, for Allison. I don't know about him."

"Did she tell you it was casual?"

"No. I assumed it was from the way she acted when she was with him. He used to meet her after work sometimes."

"When did she stop seeing him?"

"I'm not sure. He hadn't been around in a while and I asked her about him and she said he was history."

"That was when?"

"A week or so before Easter break."

"She give you any reason for the bust-up?"

"No. It wasn't any of my business."

"Is Oster a student at the university?"

"Yes."

"Live on campus or off?"

"I can't tell you that. I barely know him."

"Can you point me to anybody who does know him?"

"One of Allison's roommates, perhaps. Otherwise . . . no."

Down the block from the Unicorn was a coffee shop that had a public telephone back by the rest rooms. I looked up Gary Oster's name in the directory: no listing. I considered calling Helen McDowell, since it was nearly five o'clock, but I had nothing to tell her yet. Wait until after I'd talked to one or more of Allison's roommates, and maybe Oster, if I could find him. It would be easier on both of us if I had at least a few scraps of information to give her.

To kill some time I sat at the counter and drank two cups of coffee and paged through today's issue of the Eugene *Register-Guard.* There was nothing in the paper to hold my interest for more than thirty seconds. At five-fifteen I loaded myself into the car again and drove back through the steady rain to Hilyard. Still nobody home. So I murdered another half hour by driving over to Eugene's east-side neighbor, Springfield, and returning by way of an aimless circuit through the university campus. And this time, when I turned onto Hilyard, a car was parked in the driveway alongside the big old house—a lemon-yellow Volkswagen bug with a cluster of stickers plastered to its rear end: *Free Tibet; No Newts; Celebrate Diversity; Pro Family, Pro Child, Pro Choice.*

I parked and went up and rang the bell.

8

The young woman who opened the door (but not until I'd identified myself and held the photostat of my investigator's license up to the peephole) had plain features and a short, compact body encased in Levi's jeans and a bulky knit sweater. But she had beautiful hair: hip-length, a glossy seal-brown, parted in the center and flowing down around her face and over her shoulders. It rippled and glistened when she moved. She wouldn't lack for male attention, I thought, despite her plainness. That hair would make young fingers itch to caress it. It even gave my horny old fingers a couple of longing twinges.

Her name was Karyn Standish—"Karyn with a 'y,' " she informed me solemnly as we went into an old-fashioned front parlor stuffed with mismatched and mostly bargain-basement furniture. A CD player was giving out with fifties-style rock music by George Thoroughgood and the Destroyers. So Ms. Standish also saw fit to inform me before, mercifully, she went and lowered the volume so we could talk without half shouting at each other.

She sat in a loose-hipped sprawl in one of several chairs; I picked another, larger one that looked as though it would accommodate my weight, and did without squeezing what Kerry sometimes refers to as my "ample duff." At the end of a long, heavy sigh Ms. Standish said, "It's really weird, you know? I mean, you read about things like this, people just disappearing all of a sudden, but when it happens to one of your friends . . . wow. Weird and scary."

"Yes, it is. I understand Allison told you and your other room-mates she was driving home during Easter break, but that she didn't give you any reason."

"Just that she had a surprise for her mom. I asked her what it was but she smiled like it was a big secret and said she'd tell us all about it later."

"So as far as you knew, she was going alone?"

"Well, she didn't say one way or the other. But that's what we assumed."

"And none of you knew about her new boyfriend."

"No. Al never said a word."

"Close-mouthed about things like that, even with her room-mates?"

"Well, she talks about her love life sometimes, when she's in the right mood. Who doesn't?"

I don't, I thought. I said, "His name may be Rob."

"Her new lover? Really? Rob what?"

"No last name yet. I was hoping you might be able to supply one."

"Rob, Rob . . . You sure that's his name?"

"Not positive, but it seems probable."

"I know a couple of Bobs," Ms. Standish said. Absently she lifted both hands, splay-fingered, through her hair and then let it fall slowly—a gesture, conscious or unconscious, that was both sensuous and seductive. Light from a nearby floor lamp made it glisten with bronze highlights. "Al knows them too. But they . . . uh-uh, it couldn't be either of them. I mean, they're just not her type."

"What is her type?"

"Oh, you know, brainy like her. Cute and brainy."

"Gary Oster fit into that category?"

"Gary? Sure. Definitely."

"Allison dated him for a while, I understand."

"Two or three months."

"What happened?"

She shrugged. "They broke up."

"When, exactly?"

"I don't know *exactly.* Five or six weeks ago."

"Do you know why?"

"Al wouldn't say. But I think she blew him off."

"Because she'd met Rob, maybe."

Ms. Standish repeated the lifting gesture with her hair. "Well, it must be," she said. "Al's been going out a lot the past month or so. We all thought it was casual—you know, to get over Gary—but it could've been one guy. Somebody special."

"So special she wasn't ready to share him yet."

"Right. Keep him all to herself for a while." Two-beat, then she said as if she'd just had a tremendous insight, "I'll bet *he* was the surprise she had for her mom."

"Probably. How well do you know Gary Oster?"

The question prompted her to show me small, sharp teeth in a smile that was half ingenuous and half wicked. "Not as well as I'd like to. He's a hunk. I'm not the only one who thought Al was nuts for blowing him off."

"How did he take the breakup?"

"Pretty hard. He seemed real bitter."

"Bitter enough to hold a grudge, do something foolish?"

". . . You mean to Al?"

"Or to Rob. Or to both of them."

"Uh-uh, no way. Not Gary."

"Why not?"

"He's not like that. Not aggressive, you know?"

What I knew was that aggressions can be masked and hidden, even the most deadly kind. I asked, "Did he bother Allison in any way after the breakup?"

"What do you mean, bother her?"

"Keep calling her, keep hanging around."

"No, nothing like that."

"Would she've told you if he was giving her a hard time?"

"Me or Chris or Jan. Anyhow, we'd have *known* if he was. There's only one phone here, and one of us would've seen him if he'd been hanging outside."

"Where does Oster live, can you tell me?"

"One of the frat houses, I think. Or did he move off campus? I'm not sure."

"Does he have a job?"

"I don't think so. His dad's a doctor. He's not pre-med, though. Business major."

"Is there anyplace I might find him, somewhere he goes regularly in the evening?"

"Well, there's Porky's."

"What's that?"

"Pizza parlor over on Pearl. It's a Ducks hangout . . . you know, U of O students. I don't go much myself—I can't do pizza and beer very often with my figure—but when I do, Gary's usually there sipping suds."

Porky's was big, noisy, garishly lit, and packed. Half the customers looked to be college kids; the other half, at this hour, was a mix of adults and preteens, most of whom seemed to be regulars who were trying their damnedest to live up to the name of the place. There was enough excess body tallow distributed throughout to start a candle factory.

Gary Oster wasn't in attendance, not yet. One of the half-dozen young people manning the pizza ovens and beer spigots knew Oster and said he came in most nights by eight. I considered having my dinner there while I waited and rejected the idea immediately. Tuesday night's chicken-fried disaster was enough high-cholesterol food to last me a month.

I drove along Pearl until I found a quiet-looking restaurant with only a few cars in its lot. Roast chicken and a dinner salad gave the digestive juices something to work on, and allowed me to use up an hour in relative peace. It was a few minutes past eight when I reentered Porky's.

The joint was even noisier and more crowded now, though most of the excess tallow had been replaced by college kids who were slimmer and more energetic, if no less hungry and thirsty. Gary Oster was one of them; the employee who knew him pointed him out, sitting alone at a two-person table in the rear, a half-full pitcher of dark beer at one elbow, brooding into a mug that he had clenched between both hands. He was broad-shouldered, heavyset without being fat, and the owner of a mop of curly black hair. He didn't know I was there until I slid into the chair across from him; then his head came up, spasmodically. His eyes were dark, too, under rat's-nest brows, and bright with what I took to be a combination of hurt and smoldering anger.

"Gary Oster?"

"Who the hell're you?"

"I'd like to talk to you about—"

"Go away. I don't want to talk."

"Not even about Allison McDowell?"

He made another jerky movement, this one bowing his body forward so that his chin was almost resting on the pitcher of beer. He narrowed his eyes at me. "What do you know about Al?"

"I know she's missing."

"That's not news anymore. So?"

"So I'm trying to find her."

"What are you, a cop?"

"Private investigator." I told him my name. I tried to show him my license photostat at the same time, but he didn't have any interest in it.

"What happened to her?" he asked grimly.

"No idea yet. You wouldn't have one, would you?"

"I wish to Christ I did." He took a long swallow from his mug, refilled it from the pitcher with hands that were not quite steady. He wasn't drunk; the shaking was a product of the emotions simmering inside him. "Missing ten days and I just heard about it yesterday."

"Who told you?"

"Jan. Jan Walters, one of her roommates."

"Did you know she'd left Eugene during Easter break?"

"How would I know? Haven't talked to her in weeks, not since she—" He broke off.

"Not since she what?"

He shook his head, then banged the flat of one hand on the table hard enough to swivel heads in our direction. "Shit," he said. "Why'd she have to take up with him? Why *him*, of all goddamn guys."

"Who? Rob?"

"If he's responsible," Oster said, "if he did anything to hurt her, I'll kill the motherfucker. I swear to God I'll kill him."

"Rob?" I repeated.

"Who the hell else?"

"What's his last name?"

"Brompton. Rob fucking Brompton."

"You know him pretty well, do you?"

"Well as I ever want to know him."

"Tell me about him."

"Tell you what?"

"Where he lives, for starters."

"Over on Eighteenth. Married students' housing."

"Brompton's married?"

"No. Singles live there too." Oster made a derisive nasal sound, like a flatulence in his sinuses. "Special privileges. Oh, yeah, right."

"He live alone or with roommates?"

"One guy. Cottages aren't big enough for more than two people. Perkins, Ken Perkins. I went over there this morning to talk to him. Waste of time."

"Perkins doesn't know anything about the disappearance?"

"Said he didn't. No reason for him to lie. Two of them gone, just like that—Al and Brompton. If he did anything to her . . ."

"What's Rob Brompton like?"

"What?"

"Brompton. What's he like?"

"Smart. Four-plus GPA, dean's list . . . that's the reason Al turned on to him. Full of big-crank ideas."

"Such as?"

"Change the world. All that liberal bullshit."

"I take it you like things the way they are."

"Who says so? It's a lousy world, but committees and newsletters and protest marches aren't gonna change it. Bullshit, that's all." He sucked down more beer. "I tried to tell her. But she wouldn't listen. Just wouldn't listen."

"What did you try to tell her?"

"What she was getting into. She said I was prejudiced. I'm not prejudiced, for Chrissake. I love her, I want to marry her, I don't want to see her hurt—"

"Wait a minute," I said. "Why would Allison accuse you of prejudice?"

"Why do you think?"

"I'm asking you. I don't know anything about Rob Brompton or how Allison got involved with him. I'm blundering around in the dark here."

"Dark," Oster said bitterly. "Yeah, right."

I waited.

"Rob Brompton's black," he said.

9

The married students housing facilities on Eighteenth off Patterson had a military look, like army dormitories—probably because they had been built during World War II. Impermanent housing that became permanent as the university's enrollment grew steadily larger. Little cottages sewn together in long rows separated by blacktop lanes with narrow berms and speed bumps every few yards. Each had a peaked roof, tiny yard, tiny stoop; some sported picket fences; most seemed to have an outside array of bicycles, tricycles, strollers, kids' toys, and/or yapping dogs.

It took me a while to find the cottage shared by Rob Brompton and Ken Perkins; I had to stop and ask directions. Its uncurtained front window was lighted, the outspill showing a relatively well-tended yard. The car parked in front was a ten-year-old Datsun.

Ken Perkins turned out to be lean, studious-looking, with one of those short flattops surrounded by shaven scalp that many young African American men favor nowadays. When I identified and explained myself, he seemed eager to cooperate. Inside were two rooms and a kitchenette, all of them college-student untidy: books and papers strewn over every available surface. Perkins cleared a raggedy Goodwill chair of a sociology text and a library copy of a novel by Chester Himes and invited me to sit down.

"I don't understand how a thing like this could've happened," he said. "It was just a trip down to the Bay Area to see their people. A big deal to them but no big deal. You know?"

I nodded. "Rob's from the Bay Area too?"

"We both are. El Cerrito."

"Did he know Allison down there?"

"No. They met on campus."

"Just recently?"

"Couple of semesters ago. They had the same psych class."

"But it was recently that they became involved."

"About six weeks. They were both on the student council and they got to be friends, took to seeing each other in the evenings, and boom, they both fell hard."

"How hard?"

"The hardest," Perkins said. "That's why they decided to go home over the break, see their people—get them over the shock in person."

"Then what? Marriage?"

"That's the plan."

"Soon?"

"Not until they both graduate. But they were set to move in together this summer."

"With or without the approval of their families?"

"Right. Al thought her mother would understand, be supportive. Rob . . . well, he wasn't so sure about his people. His dad's old-fashioned." Perkins grinned wryly. "Make that bigoted. Races shouldn't mix, separate but equal, all that."

"The Louis Farrakhan philosophy."

"You got it."

"Have you talked to him about the disappearance?"

"Well, I called him the first time on Sunday. Rob and Al were supposed to be back before the end of last week, and when I didn't see or hear from them by Sunday afternoon I got worried enough to call Rob's dad."

"How come he didn't call you? He must've suspected something was wrong when Rob didn't show in El Cerrito as planned."

"He didn't know they were coming. Rob figured it'd be best if he and Al just walked in cold. He was pretty concerned then, but when I called him again yesterday, after that asshole Oster stopped by, then he was really shook up."

"Was that the first you'd heard the details, from Oster?"

"What few there are, yeah."

"Did you tell Rob's father about Allison?"

"Her being white? No. Just her name and that they were driving down together as a surprise. I didn't want to make things any harder for him. He'll find out soon enough."

"He hasn't contacted Allison's mother," I said. "Did he ask for her name and phone number?"

"Yesterday. But I couldn't remember her first name and I don't have her number. And I didn't tell him Al was from Lafayette. Dead tip she's white if I had."

"Would you mind letting me have the Bromptons' address and number? It probably won't be necessary for me to contact him, but the Lassen County authorities will want to."

"Sure, if it'll help."

"I could use a photo of Rob too."

"Ought to be one around here somewhere."

He went into the bedroom and stayed in there for three or four minutes. In one of the adjacent cottages a baby was squalling, loud enough so that the kid might have been in the room with me. Must be fun trying to study in quarters like these, I thought. Oster had said Rob Brompton was "privileged" to have gotten this housing as a minority single student. Some privilege.

Perkins came back with a three-by-five snapshot and a piece of notepaper containing the address and telephone number of Rob's parents. "Photo's of the two of us," he said. "Only one I could find."

It was a color snap, probably taken on the university campus, Perkins and Brompton with their arms across each other's shoulders, mugging a little for the camera. Rob Brompton was a nice-looking young man, large-boned and large-framed, all of his meat evenly distributed and without any trimming of fat. Medium dark-skinned, hair cropped close but without skull-shaving around the ears and above the neck. His smile was the kind once described as winning.

"This'll do fine," I said. I put the photo into my pocket with the one of Allison. "I take it you don't like Gary Oster much."

"Not much. How'd you know?"

"Well, you called him an asshole."

The wry grin again. "So I did. Exactly what he is too. What Al ever saw in him is beyond me. She's a good lady, smart, perceptive. I guess maybe he was her blind spot."

"Uh-huh."

"Rob's the one who opened her eyes," Perkins said. "Made her see that Oster's a closet racist, among other things. She wouldn't have anything more to do with him after the hassle."

"What hassle is that?"

"When she told him she was quitting him for Rob. He threw a fit. Called Rob names, called her names—ugly scene."

"Were you there?"

"No. Rob told me about it."

"Did Oster threaten either of them?"

"Not in so many words. You think maybe he had something to do with it? The disappearance?"

"Anything's possible at this stage. What's your take on the idea?"

He thought about it. "Hard to say. Maybe, if he worked himself up enough. Damn, though . . . all the way down in California . . . it doesn't seem possible he could follow them all that way, even if he found out they were going and when."

"No, it doesn't."

"But if a guy goes crazy," Perkins said, "he's capable of just about anything. All the stuff you read in the papers, all the sick shit that happens every day . . . It doesn't have to be Oster. It could be anybody, right? Somebody they didn't even know. If Rob and Al—"

He didn't finish it.

I found a motel off Highway 99, not far from the campus. In my room, first thing, I phoned Helen McDowell at home. Even though it was almost ten o'clock, she answered immediately.

"My God," she said, "I've been waiting and waiting to hear from you." The strained quality of her voice told me that she had news too. Bigger news than mine. "Allison's car. It's been found."

"Where?"

"In Eureka."

". . . Eureka?"

"Of all places. In a public parking lot downtown. It—the police said it had been there at least a week, accumulating parking tickets."

"What did they find inside?"

"Nothing to suggest . . . well, at least I still have that much to hold on to."

Nothing to suggest foul play was what she'd been about to say. "Any leads to where Allison and Rob might have gone?"

"Evidently not."

"Her luggage? His?"

"Both suitcases were locked inside. There wasn't anything in his to identify him."

"I found out who he is," I said. "That's why I called this late."

I told her about Rob Brompton—everything I'd learned except for the fact that he was black. The discovery of the abandoned MG had given her enough to deal with for the present.

She said, "Do you think . . ." and then seemed to choke on the rest of the sentence. She cleared her throat and started over, haltingly. "Do you think he . . . Rob Brompton . . . I mean, that he . . ."

"I know what you mean," I said gently. "No. My impression is that he's a good kid."

It didn't reassure her much. "Why would they go to Eureka?" she said. "I don't understand that, when they were all the way over in Lassen County."

Only one way it made sense to me, with the superficial knowledge I had, and I was not about to hurt her with it. I said, "Was it Captain Fassbinder who notified you?"

"Yes. He called at five, just as I was about to close up the shop."

Contact Fassbinder in the morning, I was thinking, tell him about Rob Brompton and see if there's anything he held back about the MG to spare Mrs. McDowell's feelings.

She said, "Will you drive to Eureka tomorrow?"

No, I thought. But I said, "I'm not sure yet."

"But if that was the last place Allison . . ."

"Whatever I do, I'll be in touch."

"All right." She made a shuddery sound. "I don't know how much more of this I can stand. I want a drink desperately, but if I have one I'm afraid I won't stop until I pass out."

What can you say? Platitudes, more empty reassurances? I muttered a lame suggestion that she try to get some rest, and broke the connection.

All the driving the past three days had fatigued me, but it was a physical tiredness only. My mind was in one of those hyperactive states where you know damned well you're going to have trouble shutting it down. No sense in going to bed yet. Instead, I went into the bathroom and ran a tubful of hot water and got in to soak and think.

Eureka. I didn't like that, not a bit; it put a new and disturbing slant on things. Eureka was on the coast, the largest town in the northern part of the state, some 250 miles west of Susanville. It didn't add up that after the MG had already broken down once, and a mechanic had warned Allison of other potential problems, she and Brompton would opt for a reverse course from Lassen County all the way over to the coast, much of the distance over rough wilderness roads. Sure, they'd made a spur-of-the-moment change in plans to take 395 downstate rather than the much faster Highway 5 route, and it was possible they'd made another impulsive decision to swing over to Eureka and follow scenic Highway 1 to the Bay Area. But given the MG's problems, and what I'd learned of Allison and Rob and their intentions, it wasn't likely.

The only other explanation, the logical one, was that they hadn't gone to Eureka; that a third party had driven the MG there. Red herring: abandon the car a long way from the real vanishing point to throw the authorities off the track.

Foul play, in that event. No question.

I ran more hot water into the tub. Gary Oster? Followed them down from Eugene, committed an act of violent revenge at some point after they'd left Creekside? Ken Perkins had pointed out a couple of obvious flaws in that reasoning, and there were others too; even without them it would be stretching credibility pretty thin. Same was true for any other person they'd known in Oregon. There was no good sense in anyone trailing them several hundred miles and then waiting around until their car broke down and was repaired before assaulting them.

Stranger or strangers, then. Allison and Rob in the wrong place at the wrong time in conflict with the wrong people.

In Lassen County, assuming they'd continued south on 395? As Fassbinder and I had discussed, it didn't have to be; they could have run into trouble anywhere in a several-hundred-mile radius stretching all the way to the Bay Area. On the other hand, there was the Eureka factor. If the MG *had* been abandoned as a red herring, it was probable Eureka had been picked because it was far away, and because it was the nearest good-sized town in which an abandoned vehicle wouldn't escape police attention for very long. The idea being that the sooner it was discovered, the sooner the focus of the investigation would shift. Not a very smart scheme: Eureka was too far away and in the wrong direction. The fact that it had taken a week for the MG to be found had also worked contrary to the plan.

So Lassen County was still the best bet. And to narrow the focus even more, there was Creekside, the last place Allison and

Rob had been seen. The unfriendly little pimple on the backside of nowhere.

I kept thinking about Rob Brompton being a black man. Nobody in Creekside had volunteered that information to me, nor, as far as I knew, to Ralph Fassbinder, and neither Fassbinder nor I had asked the right questions to bring it out. Now that I knew, certain things people had said to me on Tuesday—some subtle, some not so subtle—took on significance.

Bartholomew, at the Northern Comfort: *I never seen him. Girl came in for the room. Otherwise—*

Art Maxe: *Holding hands. Christ, even kissing on each other.* And the spitting mouth he'd made afterward.

Lena at the Modoc Cafe: *Good-looking kid, not too dark . . . Couldn't keep their hands off each other. In a place like this, in the middle of the Saturday dinner rush . . . stupid. Very stupid. Calling attention to themselves like that. These are the mountains, mister, not the big city.*

Was that the key circumstance, a good-looking young black man and an attractive young white woman forced to spend the night in a backwater like Creekside?

One resident, or more than one, taking offense and then crossing the line into violence? And some kind of conspiracy of silence as a result?

Or was there even more to it than that?

I remembered other things too, now. Maxe saying in the Eagle's Roost: *These mountains, they got secrets nobody can find out.* Lena telling me she'd seen Allison and Rob talking to two men after they left the cafe that Saturday night. The peculiar pair in camouflage fatigues and the camouflage Jeep who had nearly run me down. And the flyer that had been posted in the Creekside General Store—the flyer from the Christian National Emancipation League, an outfit "dedicated to purifying America of race-mixing and mongrelism, and to the emancipation of the white seed and the rise and rebirth of God's Chosen People."

10

I was up early again on Friday morning, on the road by seven-thirty. No rain, just broken clouds and cold winds. I drove straight down Highway 5 and reached Medford before ten. On the southern outskirts I located a service station that had a booth with a working telephone, and made two calls.

The first was to the Lassen County Sheriff's Department. Ralph Fassbinder was in and still willing to cooperate with me. He'd been in touch with the Eureka police again earlier that morning, he said; they had smudged fingerprints and no other leads from the MG or the kids' luggage. The car had been in reasonably good working order, so it hadn't been abandoned for mechanical reasons. I explained what I'd learned in Eugene, gave him the address and phone number of Rob Brompton's parents in El Cerrito. He thought they and Helen McDowell ought to be told the whole truth, meaning the interracial angle, and volunteered to do the telling. I was more than willing to leave the chore in his hands.

The down side of the conversation was that he didn't feel half as strongly as I did about the feasibility of race-related violence, or put much stock in my red-herring theory. It was plain that he believed, or wanted to believe, that Allison and Rob had driven her MG to Eureka and vanished there. Rural authorities tend to be protective of their own, and slow to give credence to acts of deadly force—hate crimes in particular—without irrefutable proof. I didn't argue with him; it would only have turned him against me, and there might come a time when I would need his support. He didn't ask if I was planning to return to Creekside, and I didn't volunteer the information that I was headed straight there.

Call number two went to my office. "I'm making some headway," I told Tamara, "but the direction it's taking isn't good." I filled her in on Rob Brompton, the discovery of Allison's MG, and the inferences I'd drawn about Creekside and its citizens.

There was a silence when I finished. Then, bitterly, "Damn niggers never learns, does they," in an exaggerated dialect. "Don't mess wif no white woman, or out come de sheets."

I let it pass. Any comment I made would only have sounded condescending.

"Well, if that's the way it is, truth's got to come out." Her normal voice, with an edge. And professional again too: "What can I do?"

"Get me specifics on an outfit called the Christian National Emancipation League. Based in Modesto, address on Milltown Road. Head of it—'grand pastor,' he calls himself—is Richard Artemus Chaffee." I spelled the last name for her.

" 'God only loves whitey' bunch?"

"Yeah. I need a better idea of what kind—how large, how active, if they have any history of violence against minorities. And if there's any direct connection between the league and anybody in Creekside, or the league and that part of the state."

"I can punch up some preliminary stuff right now, if you want to hang on . . ."

"No, take your time and put together a complete package. Talk to Joe DeFalco, if you can reach him at the *Chronicle;* find out what he knows about the league."

"Will do," Tamara said. "Want me to call you on your cell phone when I've got the package?"

"Mobile reception is lousy in the mountains. Better if I call when I get to Creekside. Is there a number where I can reach you this afternoon?"

"Right here. I'll stick around until I hear."

"I thought you had a class Friday afternoon."

"I do, but this is more important."

"Thanks, Tamara."

"Stay cool." She paused. "Maybe we'll kick some bigot ass, huh?"

"Maybe we will."

The rain clouds that had soaked Oregon the previous day had blown south into California. I picked up the stragglers just after I crossed the state line at Tule Lake, and it was raining hard enough coming through the Modoc National Forest to force my speed down to an average of forty. It was past one o'clock when I rolled into Alturas. I stopped there for gas and coffee to go, and at two-fifteen I was back in Creekside.

Dismal little place under a wet gray sky: empty streets, the collection of frame and log buildings looking huddled and oddly insubstantial, as if they were sets built for a Hollywood location shoot. You had the feeling that the lights behind their windows were skillfully placed reflector lamps, that any door you opened would lead you not into a room but into more wet, gray daylight.

I parked in front of the Creekside General Store. On the wall in front was a public phone in a plastic shell. I used it to ring Tamara's line at the office. Busy. I could have rung the other office number—the listed line—but I didn't want to interrupt her work. I hung up, went inside the store.

The same heavyset woman was alone in there, doing something in one of the cramped aisles. I paused by the door to scan the corkboard affixed to the wall. The flyer I'd torn down on Tuesday had not been replaced.

The woman came out to see who her customer was. No customer: trouble. Her eyes took on a refrigerated look. A rat in one of the produce bins would have gotten a warmer reception.

"You again," she said.

"Me again."

"I don't know any more'n I did the other day, so there's no use in bothering me. Buy something or get out."

"How about a membership in the Christian National Emancipation League?"

". . . The what?"

"There was a flyer on your bulletin board the last time I was here. Put out by the Christian National Emancipation League of Modesto. Who tacked it up?"

"How should I know? People put all kinds of crap on that board. What you think it's there for?"

"But you never noticed the flyer."

"No, I never did."

"Don't know what this league is all about."

"Mister," she said, "I don't know nothing about nothing."

But her eyes had flicked away from mine, to roam the close-packed shelves. She knew, all right. She knew about the Christian National Emancipation League and she knew who had put that particular piece of crap on her bulletin board.

The Modoc Cafe was also empty of customers. Just the cook in back and Lorraine sitting in one of the booths with a cup of coffee and a cigarette. She didn't like seeing me again any more than the woman in the general store had. Nobody in Creekside, I thought, was going to like seeing me again. Not if I could help it.

I asked her what time Lena came on; she said four o'clock. Then, "What you want with Lena?"

"Few more questions."

"About what?"

I smiled at her.

She said, "Whyn't you leave us alone, huh? Nobody knows what happened to those kids."

"Somebody knows, Lorraine. Somebody, somewhere."

She sat there, not saying anything, waiting for me to go away. I didn't go away. Pretty soon she said, "Now what?"

"A bowl of soup and a cup of coffee."

Heavy sigh. "What kind of soup?"

"What kind have you got?"

"Cream of road kill," she said.

"Is that supposed to be funny?"

"Nothing's funny around here anymore. We got split pea and chicken noodle, take your pick."

I picked chicken noodle. Another bad choice: I should've known better than to order anything swallowable at the Modoc Cafe. The coffee was bitter, the soup lukewarm and loaded with enough floating fat eyes to keep me from even sampling one spoonful; I don't like to be stared at by my food. I didn't summon Lorraine when I was ready to leave. Instead, I looked up the prices on the menu and left payment on the table. Exact amount, no tip.

"I got the shit you wanted," Tamara said. "And believe me, shit is the right word."

I shifted position, turning my back to the cold gusts of wind that blew in against the general store's front wall. I'd have preferred to make the call inside somewhere, out of the weather, but the only other public phone in Creekside was in the Eagle's Roost—too close to the bar for complete privacy.

"Go ahead."

"Christian National Emancipation League," she said. "Operating under that name for about three years, but founded ten years ago by this dude Chaffee. Used to be a salesman down in the Central Valley. Gave up his job and became a preacher in 'eighty-four, courtesy of one of those sham outfits that ordain by mail. Opened up a temple outside Turlock called Church of the Emancipator, preached a combination of fundamentalist religion and racist bullshit. Usual white-race-is-the-chosen-race garbage. Not many followers, not until he began to deemphasize religion and come down heavy on the white supremacist angle. That's when the Church of the Emancipator turned into the Christian National Emancipation League."

"How many members?" I asked.

"No way of getting an exact count. Doesn't seem to be more than about a hundred."

"What's their philosophy? Separatism through violence?"

"Not openly."

"Not a militant outfit, then?"

"Like I said, not openly. Man, these hate groups are all militant to one degree or another. Posse Comitatus, neo-Nazi Skinheads, the NAAWP, White Aryan Resistance, the fucking Klan . . . all of 'em."

"No direct surface links to violent acts or weapons offenses?"

"Not that I could find. League doesn't seem to be one of the real hard-line groups like the Aryan Brotherhood or those crazy assholes that blew up the Federal building in Oklahoma City or Butler's 'Heavenly Reich' in Idaho. But under the surface . . . who knows?"

"Did you find any connection between the league and Creekside?"

"No. None."

"Or word of league activity in Modoc or Lassen counties?"

"Same zero. Joe DeFalco's checking out that angle. By the way, he wants you to call him soon as you can. Said to tell you he'll be at his desk until five-thirty."

"He smells a story, right?"

"What else?"

DeFalco is an old-guard newspaperman, been with the *Chronicle* nearly a quarter of a century and in the game for forty years—the slide-by kind most of the time now, but high energy and tenacious as hell when it suits him. Which is when he figures he might be on to something that will benefit Joe DeFalco. The one ambition he has left is to win a Pulitzer Prize. He'll never do it—he's not that good—but it keeps him going.

For all his faults, he's a decent guy and a friend; and these days he likes me enough to do just about any favor without complaint, thanks to a fairly high-profile case I'd been involved in last fall, right after Kerry and I were married. He'd worked part of it with me, and been handed an exclusive for his help—his biggest story in years. He was still bitching about the Pulitzer committee's failure to reward him for it.

"I'll give him a buzz when I get a chance," I said. "Anything else?"

"One thing, but not about the McDowell case."

"Other business?"

"Well, you had a call just before noon. Kind of funny."

"Funny?"

"Man said his name was Eberhardt."

That stopped me cold. "My ex-partner?"

"Only Eberhardt you know, right?"

"For Christ's sake," I said angrily. "What is this, old home week? Two calls from Barney Rivera and now out of the blue, Eberhardt. Of all damn people."

"Maybe they both want the same thing."

"Yeah, maybe." Rivera had mentioned a personal matter and "a mutual friend," and now this call. Who else but Eberhardt? "What'd he say?"

"Not much. Want me to play the tape for you?"

"No." I had no interest in hearing his voice. "Just give me the gist of it."

"He asked for you and I told him you were out of town and he wanted to know when you'd be back. I said I didn't know. He tried to get me to tell him where you were but I wouldn't, not after that business six months ago. He was quiet so long I thought he was through talking, but then he asked would you be checking in sometime today. I said you would and he said tell you he'd appreciate a call back today or tomorrow, before Sunday."

"'Appreciate a call back.' Those exact words?"

"Yep. 'Tell him I'd appreciate a call back today or tomorrow, before Sunday. At my office or at home.' "

"Why before Sunday?"

"No explanation. He sounded kind of uncool."

"Uncool. Meaning what?"

"You know, hesitant, like he wasn't sure he ought to have called you up in the first place. You want his home and office numbers? He left 'em both."

"No. All right, what the hell. Go ahead."

I scribbled his office number in my notebook. He was still living in the same house on Elizabeth Street because the home number was still the same. I didn't have to write that one down. It would have taken me a lot longer than three years to forget a number I used to call two or three times a week.

"So that's it from here," Tamara said. "Anything more you want me to do?"

"No. You can go ahead and close up."

"You need me later, I'll be home tonight after six and most of the weekend."

"Okay."

"I mean it," she said. "Ring up anytime. This one's kind of personal, you know what I'm saying?"

For a couple of seconds I thought, foolishly, that she was referring to Eberhardt. The McDowell case, of course—Allison and Rob. I said I'd be in touch if I needed her, and rang off.

In the car I sat and watched the rain make tear-streak patterns on the windshield. Eberhardt. After more than three years of dead silence. A week before the wedding last fall, I'd given in to Kerry's insistence and called him at home to invite him to attend our civil ceremony at Civic Center. He hadn't been in, and I'd left a message on his machine. No return call. Kerry hadn't gotten any more satisfaction from Bobbie Jean Addison, the woman he lived with. The two of them had once been friends too, and she'd spoken briefly with Bobbie Jean on the phone, and Bobbie Jean had begged off with a lame excuse. Neither she nor Eberhardt had even bothered to send a card.

So what the hell was this?

Three-plus years since he'd walked out on our business and our friendship, for complicated reasons that I thought I understood, even sympathized with, but that nonetheless angered and hurt and saddened me. He had problems, Eberhardt did, stemming from his years as a lieutenant on the SFPD and a serious error in judgment that only he and I knew about and that had led to his early retirement. Even though we never talked about it, I was a constant nagging reminder of the down side of his life, his shortcomings and his failures. He needed to be free of me in order to go on living with himself, and so he'd gone away and opened his own agency—Eberhardt Investigative Services, offices in a seedy building in the Mission. For three-plus years he'd made a shoestring go of it, thanks in large part to the largesse of Barney Rivera, but he had no real prospects for success, and in another two months he would be sixty years old. He still hadn't married Bobbie Jean, despite the fact— or maybe because of the fact—that his plans for an elaborate wedding had precipitated our falling out. Whenever I thought about him, which was hardly at all anymore, it was in a brief and detached way, like the fishing recollections on Tuesday. Once I'd wondered if he was any happier or more content than he had been when we were together, if he'd found what he was looking for from the changes in his life. But I knew—not sensed, knew viscerally—that the answer to both questions was no.

Why the call, after all this time?

And why did he need to talk before Sunday? What could possibly have a two-day time limit?

Ring him back and ask him.

Sure. Simple. Except that I couldn't talk myself into doing it. Not now, while I was in the midst of a sensitive investigation that required my full attention, no distractions. Not now, and maybe not at all.

Too much time elapsed, too much water under the bridge. Too many slights, real or imagined. Too much baggage and too much hurt. The plain truth was, I wanted shut of Eberhardt now as much as he'd wanted shut of me those three-plus years ago. Had no desire to set eyes on him again, or to talk to him again, or, for my future peace of mind, to have him lurking like a phantom in the corners of my memory.

"Damn you, Eb," I said aloud. "Why couldn't you leave well enough alone?"

11

The blond kid, Johnny, was alone on the premises of Maxe's Garage, huddled up in the tiny office near the pumps with a space heater between him and the cold rain outside. He had been nervous in my presence on Tuesday; today he was as fidgety as a baby with a loaded diaper.

"Mr. Maxe ain't here," he said.

"That's all right. I'll talk to you."

"Me? Nothing I can tell you."

"Sure about that?"

He wouldn't make eye contact. "I'm sure."

"What're you afraid of, Johnny?"

"Not afraid of anything . . ."

"Your boss?"

"No, I told you, nothing."

"Where can I find him?"

"I dunno. He left about one o'clock."

"Went home, did he?"

"I dunno."

"Where does he live?"

Hesitation. His throat worked as if something were caught down there and he was having difficulty swallowing it.

"I can look it up," I said. "Save me the trouble."

"Spring Valley Road. Big white house."

"Where's Spring Valley Road?"

"Next block up, turn left, then right."

"Now," I said, "tell me about Ollie Ballard."

"Huh?"

"Ollie Ballard. Good friend of your boss, isn't he?"

". . . I couldn't say."

"What's he do for a living?"

"He . . . yard work, hauling . . . you know, that kind of thing."

"Where can I find him?"

"I dunno. I haven't seen him—"

"I meant where does he live."

"Spring Valley Road, only farther out. Little place past the creek. Listen . . ." But he didn't tell me what I should listen to; the rest of the sentence seemed to snag on the obstruction in his throat. His tongue made skittery movements along his upper lip. Ollie Ballard was one of the things he was afraid of; I could see it in his eyes.

"You get along with Ballard, Johnny?"

"Sure I do. I get along with everybody. Why?"

"Kind of an odd guy."

"I dunno what . . . odd?"

"Weird. That laugh of his—gives you the willies."

"Yeah," he said.

"Like he's a little crazy. You think?"

"I . . . well . . ."

"How does he feel about blacks?"

"Huh?"

"Black people. Doesn't like them, does he?"

"Jeez, how should I know how he—"

"That's why he joined the league."

Blink, blink, blink. "The what?"

"Christian National Emancipation League."

"What?" he said again.

"Come on, Johnny. You know what I mean."

"No," he said. "No, I never heard of any league."

"Sure you have. Maybe you're a member too."

"No! I don't belong to nothing."

"But Ballard does. Why lie about it?"

"I'm not lying. I never heard of a Christian League. I . . . you mean the Sentinels—"

The last word came out in a snipped-off whisper, as if he hadn't meant to say it and was trying to bite it back as it rolled out. He scrubbed a dirty hand over his face, smearing and blackening the sweat that had popped out there. He wasn't looking anywhere near me now.

I said, "Tell me about the Sentinels, Johnny."

"No. I dunno anything about them. . . ."

"We're past that point. And you're the one who brought up the name."

Headshake.

"Sentinels. A group like the league, right?"

Headshake.

"Ballard's a member—how about your boss? He one too?"

Blink, blink.

"Who else in town? How many?"

Blink. Headshake.

"How about a couple of guys who wear camouflage outfits and drive around in a camouflage army Jeep? One young, one about my age with a big hook nose like a hawk's?"

"Jesus!" he said.

"Who're they, Johnny? Tell me their—"

He came driving up out of his chair, so suddenly and with such violence that he kicked over the space heater and sent me backward a couple of quick steps to get clear. "Leave me alone! I dunno nothing, I don't want to talk about those . . . I ain't gonna talk to you anymore, just leave me alone!" He blundered past me, out into the rain, and was gone around the far corner of the garage.

Sentinels, I thought.

Some sort of affiliate or offshoot of the Christian National Emancipation League? Or another racist group entirely, maybe home grown? Well, whatever the Sentinels were, they were organized enough and bad enough to scare hell out a husky twenty-year-old kid.

Spring Valley Road was a narrow ribbon of asphalt, roughly paved and loaded with chuckholes, that curled out into thick forestland west of town. A dozen or so private homes were spaced along it close in, most of them old and moderately run-down on large parcels, flanked by barns and chicken coops and junk cars and vegetable patches and gnarly little apple orchards that looked as though they wouldn't produce much edible fruit. The rain gave all the places a dreary, forlorn aspect—not that a bright, sunny day would have done much to improve the shoddy appearance of most of them.

Poverty pocket, this whole area. Jobs at a minimum, and the ones that were available mostly low-pay and menial. Prospects for future betterment dim. A lot of people would feel frustrated, angry, psychologically as well as geographically cut off from the mainstream, and suspicious of federal, state, and local government because of their isolation. There'd be a high incidence of alcoholism; and a frontier attitude toward the right to bear arms and the need to protect families and property against outside forces; and a kind of paranoid bonding among those looking for easy answers and scapegoats for their troubles. Add all of that together, throw in a smattering of low IQs like Ollie Ballard's and a lack of adequate education, and you had the perfect breeding ground for hate groups and semisecret militia outfits.

The big white house Johnny had mentioned was among the first half-dozen closest to the village, no better and no worse in size or condition than its neighbors. I slowed when I spotted it, would have turned into its gravel drive except that the house showed no lights and I didn't see any vehicles parked in the yard. Wherever Art Maxe had gone, it wasn't home.

After half a mile the distance between the houses grew longer, and the ones I passed were smaller and poorer still. Two parcels seemed to have been abandoned, including one whose barn had collapsed in on itself in a sodden tangle of gray boards and rusted strips of sheet metal. Beyond that property's broken fencing, a narrow bridge spanned the rushing waters of a creek, possibly the same one that flowed through the village; and just beyond the creek was a sixty-foot twist of mud that led in among scrub pine to a clearing. A two- or three-room shack—you couldn't dignify it with any other name—slouched at the back of the clearing, on the stream's bank. Off to one side of it stood a tumbledown shed, and around back was what appeared to be a dog run fenced with chicken wire. Parked nose up to the shack's front porch sat a dented, primer-patched truck so old the Joads might have driven it out from Oklahoma on their quest for the promised land. Smoke, thin and torn away by the wind as soon as it appeared, poured out of a stovepipe chimney.

I stopped at the entrance to the muddy access lane, just long enough to reach under the dash, unclip the .38 Smith & Wesson Bodyguard revolver I keep there, turn the cylinder to put a live round under the hammer, and slip the gun into my topcoat pocket. An unnecessary precaution, maybe, but you don't take chances when you beard a lion in his own den, even a halfwit lion in a scruffy den like this. Then I drove on toward the shack, at a crawl because the surface was slick and offered about as much traction as a skin of ice.

I heard the dogs barking before I was halfway to where the truck was parked. At least two of them, one inside the shack and the other in the run out back. Big, too, from the racket they made. The furious barking and whining tightened the clutch of tension between my shoulder blades. I like animals and most dogs, but some breeds—the larger and more aggressive kind—make me edgy. I'd had run-ins with a couple of that variety; they were not experiences I cared to have repeated. And Ollie Ballard's mutts, whatever they were, sounded aggressive as hell.

I eased in alongside the battered truck, shut off the engine. As I set the brake and reached for the door handle, Ballard materialized in the shack's doorway. He wasn't alone: the dog that came out under the porch overhang with him was black and brown, weighed sixty or seventy pounds, and had a head like a cannonball studded with teeth. Pit bull. The worst damn kind of attack dog there is. My stomach kicked a little, but I didn't hesitate in climbing out. Never show fear to an animal or to a man.

The pit bull barked and growled and bared more of its canine dentalry. Ballard said something to it sharply, and it shut up and sat on its haunches and glared at me as I came around the front of the car. I stopped there and said to Ballard, "Okay if I come up out of the rain?"

He made a loose come-ahead gesture. I went up three rickety stairs slowly, my right hand in my coat pocket and my fingers touching the .38. When I moved ahead under the slanted roof I was about five feet from him and the pit bull. Too close, but I stayed put and tried to look more relaxed than I felt.

Both Ballard and the dog peered at me out of red-rimmed eyes. Behind the shack, the other animal kept on barking its fool head off—another pit bull, probably. Ballard hadn't shaved in two or three days; yellowish stubble spiked his cratered cheeks. Baggy pants and a faded and torn plaid shirt covered his stickman frame. Made for scaring crows and little children, I thought. With him around, every night was Halloween.

"You're that guy from the city," he said. "That detective. I thought you went away."

"I did. Now I'm back."

"What for? What you want here?"

"Looking for Art Maxe."

"Art? I ain't seen him since yesterday."

"Know where I can find him?"

"Nah. Garage or home, likely."

"He's not either place."

"What you want with Art anyway?"

"Ask him some more questions."

"About that girl and her nigger? He already told you, he don't know what happened to 'em."

"How about you?"

"Huh? Me?"

"You know what happened to them, Ballard?"

"Shit, no. Wouldn't tell you if I did."

"Didn't like it much, did you."

"Huh?"

"White woman, black man."

"Goddamn right I didn't like it. Pretty little piece like her, letting that nigger do her. Made me want to puke."

"That all it made you do?"

"Huh?"

"Teach them a lesson, maybe? Hurt them?"

He stared at me with his mouth open.

"You and the other Sentinels," I said.

Five more seconds of stare. Then the high-pitched giggle came out of him, so sudden and shrill that I jerked involuntarily and the pit bull started a low, rumbling growl deep in its massive chest. It sat there growling and quivering, its hot red eyes on my throat. I closed my hand around the .38, slipped my index finger through the guard and against the cold curve of the trigger.

"What the fuck you talkin' about?" Ballard said.

"The Sentinels. You and the Sentinels."

He looked confused, but not because he didn't understand what I was saying; you could almost hear what few gears he had grinding away in his head. "What're you, a joker?" The giggle again, not as shrill. "Man, *I'm* the joker around here. Couple of aces missing, but the joker's still in the deck."

"Nothing funny about this, Ballard."

"Funny about what?" he said. Then he shook his head and said, "Three things I like and that's beer, dogs, and pussy. Sometimes I drink so much of the first, I get the last two mixed up."

"Sentinels do something to the kids? You do something?"

A little more of the openmouthed stare. His lower lip was wet with spittle. At the same time, he closed his mouth and dropped a hand to catch hold of the pit bull's collar. The dog tensed and the growling modulated into another teeth-baring snarl; I could see muscles rippling along its back, its jawline, in all four legs.

"Oughta set him on you," Ballard said. "Yeah. Rip your fuckin' throat out."

I took the gun from my pocket, not too fast because the last thing I could afford was to have it snag on the cloth. Ballard's bloodshot eyes rounded when he saw it; a thin slugline of spit wiggled down from a corner of his mouth.

"Let go of that collar," I said, "and I'll shoot him. I mean it. Him, and then you."

He didn't say anything. But his hand tightened on the collar.

"All right. I'm leaving now. But I'll be around. If you did hurt those kids, if anybody else around here did, I'll find out about it. And don't get any ideas about coming after me—it won't do you any good. I don't push around, and I'm not the only one who knows about the Sentinels. You understand me?"

His answer was another giggle.

I backed over to the steps, watching the dog and Ballard's hand on its collar. Down the steps at the same slow pace, into the wind-whipped rain. Nothing happened except that I stepped into a puddle with one of my brand-new eighty-dollar shoes. Inside the car, I locked all the doors before I laid the .38 on the seat beside me. The scarecrow and the pit bull stood still, staring like a pair of bogies, as I started the engine and backed up and went away from them.

On the ride into the village I kept thinking that I'd handled things badly with Ballard, pushed him too hard. He didn't worry me, but whoever else was mixed up in this—the Sentinels as a group or individuals among them—did. You can't guard against unknowns. I'd probably stirred up a hornet's nest by coming at Ballard the way I had; so the prudent thing to do, if I wanted to avoid being stung, was to leave Creekside again right now and establish myself at a safer distance.

The problem with that was, you can't accomplish nearly as

much from a distance as you can at close quarters. Besides, nobody had ever accused me of being prudent. I was like that pit bull: give me something worth attacking and I'd keep after it until I tore it apart.

The courtyard at the Northern Comfort Cabins was empty except for thirty or forty glistening rain puddles. I angled in close to the office, with the driver's side nearest the entrance so I would need to take only a couple of steps to get inside. It was raining as hard now as it had been in Eugene the day before—thick, wind-driven lancets out of gray-black clouds that seemed to hang just a few hundred feet about the village. The low overcast made me think of Joe Btfsplk, the character in "Li'l Abner" who had a cloud of gloom and doom hanging over him everywhere he went. If any single impression of Creekside and its citizens stayed with me, this would be it. A real-life Dogpatch with an entire population of Joe Btfsplks.

At first I thought the office was untenanted, but as I approached the counter a female head covered with stringy, gray-streaked hair came into view behind and below it. The face under the hair was round and puffy and sagging, as if all the flesh were slowly rotting away beneath the skin. One of the reasons, or likely the main reason, was gin: she had a glass of it in one hand and the air in the too-warm room was ripe with the juniper berry smell. She was sitting in an ancient cushioned armchair with her feet up on a stool. Beside her on the chair's wooden arm lay an old Bible; and in front of her, next to the door into the rear living quarters, was a portable TV with its screen dark. She might have been anywhere between forty and sixty, round and flabby and fat-ankled, wearing a shapeless Hawaiian muumuu of the sort that had gone out of style twenty-five years ago.

I leaned on the counter. "Mrs. Bartholomew?"

"Ruth Bartholomew, that's me." Raspy voice, unfuzzied by

the gin. She was the kind of heavy drinker, I thought, who would sound completely lucid right up to the moment she passed out. "Who're you?"

I told her. There was a change in her eyes—a darkening, a shifting, almost a retreating. Up came the glass; down went the rest of the gin it contained, a good two fingers. She didn't even blink.

"Well?" she said. "Why'd you come back?"

"Just doing my job. Your husband around?"

"No. Went down to Susanville. You want to stay here again?"

"If you have a vacancy."

Either the irony escaped her or she chose to ignore it. "Got nothing but vacancies this time of year. You care which one?"

"Same as before. Eleven."

She didn't comment on that. Nor did she get up out of her chair. "Seventy-five a night," she said. "In advance."

"It was fifty, three days ago."

"New rates." Her eyes challenged me to argue.

I didn't give her the satisfaction. On the counter was a stack of registration cards; I took one and filled it out. Ruth Bartholomew watched me with her gin-bright eyes, but still she made no move to stand up.

I said, "You want me to fill out the credit card slip too?"

"I'll do it. Reach the key yourself, though."

I took the key off a rack at one end. She moved then, in a series of slow pushings and liftings that were almost like a parody of the ritual movements of aikido or tai chi. I waited until she was on her feet before I said, "What can you tell me about Allison McDowell and Rob Brompton?"

"Who?"

"You know who I mean. His name is Rob Brompton."

"That so?" One of her hands gobbled up my MasterCard; it was the fastest I'd seen her do anything except suck down the gin. "Well, I don't know nothing more'n Ed told you."

"But you did see both of them while they were here?"

"I saw 'em."

"Talk to either one?"

"No."

"What'd you think about them staying here together? Black man, white woman. Unmarried."

Her mouth thinned down. "Lord's business, not mine."

"So it didn't bother you?"

"Didn't say that."

"Then it did bother you."

"Didn't say that neither. I got nothing against niggers."

"No, of course not. Your husband either, right?"

"Well?" she said. "What're you harping on that for? The race thing. What's that have to do with them two wandering off someplace, getting their fool selves lost?"

"Maybe they didn't wander off and get themselves lost."

"No? What'd they do, then?"

"Ran into some trouble, could be. Right here in Creekside."

"What trouble?"

"With some people who aren't good, tolerant Christians like you and your husband."

"Nonsense," she said. "Wasn't no trouble the night they stayed here, nor the morning they left."

"They have any visitors that night?"

"Visitors? Who'd visit them?"

"So nobody did."

"I don't spy on my guests."

"Allison called her mother long distance," I said. "She or Rob make any other calls from here? Local or long distance?"

"No."

She finished scratching numbers on the credit card slip; slapped it and my MasterCard down in front of me. I signed the slip, pocketed my copy and the card.

"Nice talking to you, Mrs. Bartholomew."

"You think so?" she said.

I smiled at her, the old wolf smile; she didn't react. At the door I stopped and turned and indulged in a little more hard pushing, to see if I could get a shove in return. "One more thing. Who do I talk to about the Sentinels?"

She was on her way through the doorway back there, probably heading after more gin; the words halted her, stiffened her back. She half turned before she said, "The what?"

"The Sentinels. Or the Christian National Emancipation League. I'll settle for either one."

Good push, but not much answering shove. She said, "I don't have no idea what you're talking about," and left me alone with the lie.

12

It was four-fifteen when I drove down from the motel and put the car into one of the angled spaces before the Modoc Cafe. The outspill of light through the cafe's plate glass window laid a saffron tint on the gathering twilight. In close to the glass, the curtain of rain had a burnished silver cast.

Lena was on duty now, Lorraine nowhere in evidence. A man and a woman sat in the last of the left-hand row of booths; they were the only customers. I claimed the first of the right-hand booths. Lena took her time coming over to me, and when she did she left her professional smile behind. But there was no hostility in her expression. Just a guarded blankness, like an empty house with its security alarm switched on.

"Persistent, aren't you," she said.

"I get paid to be."

"Maybe you don't know it, but this isn't a good place to be persistent in. Creekside, I mean."

"And why is that?"

"People here don't like pushy outsiders."

"Who keep asking questions about things nobody wants to talk about."

"That's right."

"How about you? What do you think of pushy outsiders?"

"I think I don't want to answer any more of your questions."

"Not even to save a couple of lives?"

"If those kids are still alive."

"You think they might not be?"

"I didn't say that. I hope they are."

"So do I. So do their families."

Small silence. Then she asked tentatively, as if she were leery of the answer, "Where've you been the past couple of days?"

"Oregon. Being persistent."

"Do you any good?"

"Some. You were right about the boyfriend's name—it's Rob. Rob Brompton. Not casual between them, either. They're planning to be married."

"Doesn't surprise me, I guess."

"But you don't approve?"

"Marriage is a shitty proposition when both people belong to the same race. Black and white makes it twice as shitty."

"They don't think so. It's their mistake anyway, if it is a mistake."

"Sure. I made a couple myself and neither of mine was any darker than vanilla ice cream. So why'd you come back here from Oregon? What's here for you?"

"The truth, maybe."

"What truth?"

I shrugged and said nothing, watching her.

"They disappeared here or close by, that how you figure it?"

"That's how I figure it."

Lena nibbled at her lower lip, the way you do when you're trying to make up your mind about something. Pretty soon she said, "You gonna order? Can't keep sitting here if you don't."

"Milk. Low-fat." Not even the Modoc could screw up a glass of milk.

She went away, came back with the milk. And with something else for me too: conscience and innate decency had won out over fear and self-interest, for a change.

"That Saturday night," she said, leaning close so she could be sure her voice wouldn't carry, "just after the kids left, Mike Cermak came in. He passed right by them and the two men they were talking to out front."

"Two men. You're certain of that now?"

"That much I am."

"The men wouldn't have been wearing camouflage fatigues, would they? One young, one about my age with a big hooked nose. Father and son, possibly."

Her eyes narrowed. "I can't tell you what they looked like. I wasn't lying when I said it was dark and the window was fogged up."

"Was a pair like that in the cafe that night?"

"I don't remember."

"You know the ones I described, though."

"No, I don't." Which was yet another Creekside lie. She knew, all right.

"Rough trade," I said. "I had a little run-in with them the other night."

"Is that so."

She wasn't going to talk about them no matter how much I prodded her; her eyes and her pursed mouth made that plain. If they were Sentinels, and I had a hunch they were, it meant that she wouldn't talk about the organization, either. No use in even bringing up the name. Pressure her too hard and she would curl up inside her protective shell, shut me out entirely. Conscience and innate decency go only so far in this fear-ridden, cover-your-ass society of ours.

I said, "Let's get back to Mike Cermak. You're pretty sure he saw who Allison and Rob were talking to?"

"He must have. He's not blind."

"How does Cermak feel about answering questions from outsiders?"

"He's an outsider himself," Lena said. "At least, he wasn't born up here and he keeps to himself. Mike's okay."

"Where can I find him?"

"He lives up at the top of Lodgepole Lane. Last house where it dead-ends."

"Lodgepole Lane is where?"

"Back toward the highway, south. Turn right."

"Okay to use your name with him?"

"You'd better, if you want him to talk to you. He—"

She stopped talking because the front door opened and the wet wind blew in a trio of men in their forties, none familiar to me. Lena knew them and she didn't seem to want them to know she'd been having a conversation with me; she waved and called out names, moved off in their direction without another glance in mine.

I finished my milk and went out into the coming night.

Like Spring Valley Road, Lodgepole Lane was narrow and riddled with tire-snaring potholes. It climbed onto the hillside above the village, and by the time I reached its terminus, after about a third of a mile, it was so pinched in by evergreens, two normal-sized cars couldn't have passed each other without swapping paint scrapes.

The only house up there was built on a couple of acres of cleared ground behind a crazy-quilt fence that was part grapestake, part chicken wire, and part rough-wood poles. Typical Creekside home: old, badly in need of paint and a new roof. It seemed also to list a few degrees to the south, as if it had been pushed that way by a long succession of winter storms. Lights in its facing windows pressed palely against the early darkness. The yard in front and around on one side was an incredible clutter of things spread out under tin-roofed lean-tos: car parts, tools, stacks of firewood, lengths of pipe, plumbing fixtures, appliances, hundreds of other items less easily identifiable in the gloom. A homemade sign on the gate read: CERMAK'S BARGAINS—BUY, SELL, TRADE—FREE PICKUP AND DELIVERY.

The man who opened the door to my knock was not quite a stranger: he was the aging, uncommunicative hippie I'd tried to brace at the general store on Tuesday. He didn't look any more cooperative tonight. Not hostile, just carefully neutral—like Switzerland. The hear-no-evil, see-no-evil type.

"Mike Cermak?"

Small reluctant nod.

"Remember me?" I said. "I'm the man who—"

"I know who you are. What do you want?"

"A few minutes of your time."

"I can't help you, man. I know nothing from nothing."

"Maybe you know more than you think. Lena down at the cafe said you'd talk to me. How about it?"

"Talk about what?"

"Week ago Saturday night. The two missing college kids were out front of the cafe, having a conversation with two men, when you showed up. You walked right by them."

"So?"

"So maybe you can tell me who the men were and what the conversation was about."

I watched him fret over the wisdom of compromising his neutrality. Then, "All right, come inside. Too damn cold out here." Still reluctant, but leaning the right way.

The interior of the house had the same junk-shop clutter as the front yard—a mix of private possessions and goods for sale, complete with price tags. A wood-burning stove made the place too warm. A fattish woman with long, braided hair sat on a scruffy sofa, making something that looked to be a beadwork purse. Cermak gestured to her and she got up without a word and left the room, taking her beadwork and a half-full glass of wine with her.

Cermak said to me, "I can't tell you their names."

"The two men who were talking to the kids?"

"Yeah."

"Can't or won't tell me?"

"Can't. Don't know who they were."

"They don't live around here? Strangers to you?"

". . . Not exactly strangers."

"So they do live in the area."

No answer.

"Do you know where I can find them?"

This time I got an evasion: "Won't do you any good to look them up."

"No? Why not?"

"They won't talk to you."

"Why won't they?"

"Just won't."

"Were they hassling the kids?"

"Some," Cermak said. "Bad scene."

"The white and black thing?"

"Yeah."

"Taunts, threats—what?"

"Taunts. Called him a nigger and worse."

"How did he respond?"

"Didn't respond. She wanted to argue, defend him, but the black kid hustled her away."

"The men follow them?"

"No. Yelled some more shit and then got in their Jeep and split."

"Jeep? What kind of Jeep?"

He shrugged. "A Jeep."

"Open military style. Camouflage paint job?"

"Yeah."

"Describe the men for me."

"Young. Big and young."

"Both of them?"

"Both, yeah."

"What were they wearing?"

Another hesitation. Getting information out of him was like cleaning layers of paint off an old table: you scraped and scraped but it would come off only in little chips and flecks. "Soldier shit," he said finally. "Camouflage fatigues, combat boots."

"Armed?"

"I didn't see any guns."

"Sentinels," I said. "They were members of the Sentinels, weren't they?"

A muscle twitched in Cermak's cheek. He went to where another half-full glass of wine sat on an end table; drained the glass before he looked at me again.

"What do you know about the Sentinels?"

"Not as much as I'm going to," I said. "What do *you* know about them?"

"Nothing, man. None of my business."

"They're racists. That makes them everybody's business."

"Not mine. Different universes."

"I'll bet you didn't feel that way in the sixties. I'll bet you did a little civil rights marching back then. Vietnam protests, ban-the-bomb protests."

"The sixties are dead, man," he said, "a long time dead. I'm older and smarter now."

"Older anyway."

"No bullshit lectures, all right? You don't know me and I don't know you."

"But you do know the Sentinels."

He avoided my eyes again, poured himself more wine. But sooner or later I was going to scrape off enough chips and flecks to find out what I wanted to know, and we both knew he was going to let it happen. Otherwise he wouldn't have let me into his house in the first place.

I said, "Back to a week ago Saturday night. You see the kids again after the hassle?"

"No."

"The next morning? Anytime since?"

"No."

"How about the pair in the Jeep?"

"No," Cermak said. "They don't come into town much, don't mix with the locals."

"Who doesn't? The Sentinels?"

"Those assholes were just passing through to the highway, or maybe making an emergency buy at the hardware store. It stays open late on Saturdays."

"Passing through from where?"

Silence.

"Come on, Mike, where do the Sentinels hang out? Some kind of wilderness outpost, is that it?"

Cermak worked on his wine. And then, as if the fabric of his indifference had suddenly ruptured, he blew out breath in a hissing sigh and said harshly, "Screw it. All right, yeah, they got a camp back in the woods. Big place, started building it about a year and a half ago."

"Where in the woods?"

"End of Timberline Road. Seven, eight miles west."

"Sounds like you've been there."

"Once. They bought a bunch of stuff from me before I knew who they were and I delivered it. I should've known when they gave me the goddamn badge."

"Badge?"

"Blue and white triangle. Show it at the gate, wear it on the grounds. Everybody in there wears one."

"What kind of place is it?"

"Hard to describe. They'd only gotten started on the construction when I was there. Cabins, prefab buildings . . . looked like it was going to be big. A big bad bummer."

"How do you mean?"

"One of the things they were laying out was a parade ground. Guys in fatigues—I could just see them goose-stepping around in formation once it was finished."

"Neo-Nazi?"

"I didn't see any swastikas or shit like that. But yeah, that was the impression I got. Paramilitary for sure."

"Fences? Weapons?"

"Plenty of fencing all around. Only weapon I saw was on the guard at the front gate. Assault rifle. But you can bet they've got a stash."

"How many people living there?"

"Couple of dozen back then. Lot more than that by now."

"All men?"

"Mostly. But I saw a couple of women, and one kid about ten. Families, indoctrinate 'em young. Jesus."

"Who'd you deal with?"

"Guy named Slingerland. Forty, blond, real Aryan type."

"Was he the one in charge?"

"Didn't seem that way. Somebody called the Colonel. Never heard his name."

"Fifties, bull-necked, nose looked like a hawk's?"

Cermak shrugged. "He wasn't pointed out to me. I don't remember anybody looked like that, but it was a long time ago." One corner of his mouth twisted. "And I smoke a lot of dope."

"The name Richard Artemus Chaffee mean anything to you?"

"No."

"He's head of an outfit called the Christian National Emancipation League."

"Oh, yeah. Racist flyers all over the place."

"But you're not aware of any connection between the Sentinels and this league."

"No."

"Who owns the land the Sentinels camp is on?"

He shook his head. "Used to belong to a big cattle rancher. For all I know it still does."

"What's the rancher's name?"

"Duquesne. George Duquesne."

"Know anything about him?"

"Not much. Strictly low-profile."

"So he could be one of them."

"Wouldn't surprise me."

"And the Sentinels have been recruiting locals, right? Holding open meetings, preaching racism?"

"Not openly. Clandestine stuff, word of mouth." Another lip-twist. "Whispers in the dark."

"They seem to be having much success?"

"More than you'd think. You can sell any kind of shit to some of the poor stupid schmucks up here."

"Ollie Ballard, for instance."

"That creep."

"Who else in Creekside?"

Cermak balked at that. "Gave you enough names. Christ, man, my old lady and me got to live here. No more questions. How about you split now and leave us alone?"

The fabric of his indifference had reknitted; he had it wrapped around him again—a cocoon of self-protection. Flower child grown old and gone to seed. Dropped out a long time ago and determined to stay that way: drink wine and smoke dope with his old lady, sell his bargains, and let the rest of the world slide by. But there was still a little love and caring left in him, still a little of the old sixties philosophy. Hell, by Creekside standards he and Lena were right up there with Mother Teresa in the humanitarian department.

I said, "Fair enough. Just tell me how to get to Timberline Road and the Duquesne ranch."

He told me. And that was all he had to say until he'd ushered me outside. Then, with a kind of self-mockery, "Peace, brother," and he shut the door in my face.

13

Joe DeFalco said eagerly, "Sentinels, eh? Son of a bitch. Sounds like you're on to something up there—something that could be big."

"Yeah. Name ring any bells?"

"One little chime. Title of the monthly bulletin Chaffee puts out in Modesto is *The Sentinels of Light.* Could be a coincidence, though. White supremacists love names like Sentinels, Watchdogs, Guardians."

"Or there could be a tie to the Christian National Emancipation League."

"That too. These buggers are always splitting off and forming new cells, like goddamn amoeba germs."

A gust of wind blew rain in against the side of my face; I hunched deeper inside Pac Bell's plastic shell. I'd tried to call DeFalco from my car phone—I was damn sick of the Creekside General Store—but the weather and the mountains and the distance made it impossible to get a clear connection. Even on this public phone his voice sounded far away and now and then a word or two would be lost in crackling static.

"See what you can find out, will you?"

"Damn straight I will," he said. "Let's have the rest of what you know about the paramilitary camp."

I repeated the gist of what I'd gotten from Mike Cermak.

"How long has it been operating?"

"About a year and a half, evidently."

"Population growing? Recruiting locals on the QT?"

"Looks that way."

"That's how Butler got started in Hayden Lake. And the Aryan Brotherhood at Whidby Island up in Washington State. Indoctrination centers and militia and terrorist training grounds. Your source give you any idea who's in charge up there?"

"Somebody called the Colonel. No name yet."

"Description?"

"I can't be sure," I said, "but I think he may be about our age, neck like a bull's, craggy features, long hooked nose. Probably ex-military."

"No surprise there. Lot of anarchists came out of one branch or another."

"They got the land they're using from a local rancher—" I broke off because a four-by-four with its high beams on had come along Main and was turning in next to my car. Ford Bronco, black, with a curled-back CB antenna. "Hold on a second, Joe."

"Why?"

"Company."

The driver was the Bronco's only occupant. He was fat, bare-headed, bald, and familiar—Frank, the blowhard who'd tried hassling me in the Eagle's Roost on Tuesday. He slammed the door, looked at my car, squinted up at where I stood, then climbed up next to me and looked at me some more, the way you'd look at a pile of manure on a hot afternoon.

Ah, hell, I thought, here we go again. I shifted the phone to my left hand and watched him watch me. "Something you want?"

"Why'd you come back? You ain't wanted here."

"I like the friendly atmosphere."

"Don't fuck with me. I'll rip your face off."

"Sure you will."

"Try me and see, dickhead."

I laid the receiver on the little shelf under the phone, wiped my hands along the front of my coat. "Time to crap or get off the pot, Frank."

"What?"

"You heard me. Go ahead, make trouble, see what you can do about ripping my face off."

He didn't like that; he wasn't used to challenges any more than he'd been used to being put on the defensive. "I told you, don't fuck with me. I got ten, twelve years on you, pops."

"And fifty pounds, all of it lard. Well? Make your move."

"Listen—"

"What's the matter, Frank? Afraid it's your face that'll get ripped? I'll bet you don't like seeing your own blood—a lot of your own blood."

He tried a lip curl and a snarl, took a sudden step toward me with his hands up like a boxer's. I didn't move or flinch. The uncertainty that had stopped him Tuesday night stopped him again now. He made an effort to stare me down, but that's a game I've played too often, with men twice as tough as him. He couldn't have won if we'd locked eyes for an hour.

He gave it up pretty quick. "The hell with you," he said—another lame exit line—and clumped away into the store.

I picked up the receiver. "Still there, Joe?"

"Still here. What was that all about?"

"You heard?"

"Some of it. 'Go ahead, make trouble.' Christ, you sounded like Clint Eastwood."

"Yeah, well, that's the only language assholes like this one understand."

"Who the hell was he?"

"Somebody else who objects to me poking around. I'm not making any friends up here. Where were we?"

"Sentinels," DeFalco said. "Some local rancher they got the land from."

"His name's Duquesne, George Duquesne. That mean anything to you?"

"Not offhand. I'll check him out. What . . ." The rest of the sentence got torn up by a burst of static.

"I didn't get that."

"I said what about the local authorities? You talk to them yet?"

"Not about the Sentinels. Couple of discussions with the Lassen sheriff's captain in charge of the missing persons investigation."

"Get along with him all right?"

"Reasonably."

"Then you'd better go talk to him again."

"I intend to. But I don't think he'll want to get into it yet. There's no proof to tie the Sentinels or the Christian National Emancipation League to the disappearances, and he's the type who'll demand hard evidence before he acts."

"So then what do you do?"

"I don't know yet. Keep stirring the pot."

"Clint Eastwood on the prod," he said. "Listen, if this crowd is the Hayden Lake or Whidby Island kind, they don't mind killing people. May already have gone that route . . . you know what I mean."

"I know what you mean. If you're trying to tell me to take it easy, don't do anything reckless—I hear you. I'm not Eastwood and I'm not suicidal. You be home tonight?"

"After nine. Interview I can't back out of after I leave the *Chron*. I'll be home all weekend too—me and my trusty Compaq, taking trips down the information highway. And don't call just to pump me. If this thing is as big as it sounds, I want a chunk of it. Another exclusive like that Chehalis business last fall."

"I figured."

"Okay. One more thing before I let you go—"

"Hold it, Joe."

The fat guy was coming out of the store. He stopped again a few feet from me, at the head of the steps, and mauled me with his little pig eyes while he opened a package of cigarettes. I mauled him in return. Silly, all of this macho crap, but circumstances make it necessary sometimes. Each situation has its own set of rules; you learn to recognize and adapt to them.

Frank fired up one of the cancer sticks, threw the burning match in my direction. When I didn't react, he went down to his Bronco and slammed himself inside. He made a lot more noise driving off.

I said into the phone, "Okay now."

"Same guy as before?"

"Same guy. Go ahead with what you were going to say."

"It's a question. And you won't like it."

"Just make it quick. I'm freezing my fat here."

"You have a chance to get in touch with Eberhardt?"

Eberhardt again. "Goddammit," I said. "How'd you know he called my office?"

"Tamara. She talked to him right before she buzzed me this morning."

Thank you, Ms. Corbin. But there was no reason she shouldn't have mentioned it to DeFalco; she knew he and Eberhardt had once been friends too, that Eb had shut him out in the same cold way he had me. The only reason we could figure for it was that the three of us had once been tight, in the days when we'd made up part of a weekly poker game, and Eberhardt had decided he might as well burn more than just one bridge. Not all his old bridges, though—not the link to Barney Rivera. Just the ones that didn't do him any professional good.

I said shortly, "I haven't had time."

"But you are going to call him?"

"Hell, I don't know. I haven't made up my mind yet."

"What do you figure's on his? After all this time?"

"What am I, a mind reader?"

"Don't tell me you're not curious."

"Not as curious as you seem to be. Why don't *you* call him?"

"Not my place. Maybe he . . ."

More static. When it cleared, I said, "I got to get moving. Later tonight, Joe. Or early tomorrow."

"Anytime. Listen, I mean it about getting back to Eb. I think you . . ."

Crackle, crackle. I took the opportunity to mutter a good-bye and hang up.

I made one more call, this one from the car phone because it was short distance. Ralph Fassbinder was on duty and came on the line right away. But he was busy, he said, and couldn't talk for long. I told him that what I had to say was better laid out in person anyway, and that it needed to be soon—later this afternoon or sometime this evening. He made an effort to put me off until morning, but when I insisted, he agreed to meet me at seven o'clock, at a tavern called Ron's, where he liked to have a beer before he went home. I said I'd buy.

I got the car started, drove back to the Northern Comfort. I was chilled and my clothes felt damp; I wanted a shower, and the feel of fresh underwear and my last clean shirt and pair of slacks. The only car on the lot was the Bartholomews' tired old Buick, Ed having made it home from Susanville. With a fresh load of gin for mama? I wondered if he lapped it up too—the two of them sitting in there night after night, waiting for customers, waiting for summer, drinking gin and reading passages aloud from the Bible.

The crusty old plumbing didn't let me have much hot water, as per usual, and what there was of it was discolored by minerals. The shower still felt pretty good. I put on the dry clothing and lay down on the bed under the off-center painting of Christ with his crown of thorns. I thought about calling Kerry, just to hear her voice, but it was too early for her to be home and I didn't want to bug her at the office, where she was probably still tearing her hair over the "Shirt Happens" account. I thought about following DeFalco's advice and contacting Eberhardt too, but not for more than ten seconds. Instead, I got Mrs.

Bartholomew on the phone and gave her the In the Mode number in Lafayette.

Keeping my promise, that was all: I had nothing I was willing to tell Helen McDowell yet, nothing she'd want to hear anyway. The conversation lasted about two minutes and didn't do either of us any good. I wondered as I hung up if Ruth Bartholomew had listened in. She was the type. But if she had, she was disappointed. All she'd heard were expressions of pain, emptiness, and fading hope.

I lay for a few minutes listening to the rain beat on the roof. The Sentinels . . . Creekside . . . the disappearance of Allison and Rob. The three were interconnected—I was sure of it. But in what way exactly? Those two young soldier types Cermak had seen talking to the kids, I thought. They could've come back later that Saturday night, or on Sunday morning in time to follow the MG out of town and waylay it someplace else. Or they could have reported the presence of a white woman and a black man to the Colonel, and he'd dispatched other soldiers to do the waylaying. Mindless, knee-jerk racial violence, either way—and all too possible if the Sentinels were what they seemed to be.

And yet I couldn't fit the MG's abandonment in Eureka into that kind of scenario. Why run the risk of driving the car all the way over there? Too great a distance and too unnecessary; out of character for a paramilitary outfit. The Sentinels were covert but not all the way underground, not if they were more or less openly recruiting locals; and with nothing to tie them or their camp directly to the missing kids, there was no need for a fancy red herring. If they'd killed Allison and Rob, wouldn't they have just buried or hidden the car along with the bodies, someplace deep in the wilderness?

There was more to the disappearances than execution murder by a group of white supremacists. I felt it—the kind of strong, sixth-sense hunch a person in my business learns to trust—but I couldn't come up with a scenario, given the facts I had gathered so far, that made any better sense. . . .

I was still working with the facts, shifting them around like puzzle pieces, when an engine revved up loud outside on the courtyard. Tires crunched and slid on gravel. I hoisted myself off the bed and got to the window just as somebody hurried up and began hammering on the door. I peeled back a corner of the shade to see who it was.

Art Maxe. Wearing an oilskin slicker, his dark face scowling under a plastic-covered hat. Behind him, slewed up at an angle, was a wide-body Dodge pickup. Even though the window glass and the truck's windshield were rain-streaked, I could see a brace of rifles mounted conspicuously—deer-hunter fashion—inside the truck's cab.

I opened the door. Maxe said, "I hear you been looking for me." His tone and his expression were both hostile, but it wasn't the same kind of aggressive, hate-backed hostility as Fat Frank's. Not yet, anyway.

"Ballard tell you that? Or Johnny?"

"Don't matter who told me. What're you after this time?"

"Same thing as before," I said. "You want to talk standing out there, or inside, where it's dry?"

"I ain't gonna be here long. I already told you everything I know. So quit dogging me, you hear?"

"Or else what?"

His answer to that was no answer at all. "Shit," he said.

"Fact is, you didn't tell me everything you know."

"Hell I didn't."

"You didn't tell me Allison's boyfriend is black. And you didn't tell me about the Sentinels."

Nothing at all this time. All he did was stand there with rain dripping off his hat, staring at me.

"How about it, Maxe?"

"How about what? The Sentinels? Why should I have said anything about that bunch? I got nothing to do with them."

"No?"

"No."

"But you do belong to the league."

"The what?"

"Christian National Emancipation League."

"Them neither. Listen," he said, "I don't belong to no group or organization, not even the goddamn Better Business Bureau."

"Have it your way. But you know what they are, the Sentinels and the league. You know which of your friends and neighbors belong."

"They mind their business and I mind mine. Why in hell don't you do the same?"

"My business right now is what happened to Allison McDowell and Rob Brompton."

"And you figure the Sentinels for that? Bullshit."

"She's white, he's black, and they're a pack of racists. How does that add up for you?"

"It don't add up no way. Nothing happened to those kids in this town. Nothing!"

I kept silent, prodding him with my eyes.

Pretty soon he said, "Who told you about the Sentinels?"

"I'm a detective, remember? And secrets in these mountains aren't as hard to find out about as you claimed. Is Ballard one of them?"

". . . One of what? A goddamn secret?"

"A Sentinel. Your old pal Ollie Ballard."

"Ollie's no friend of mine."

"Two of you seemed pretty friendly the other night."

"A beer now and then, that don't make us buddies. You think Ollie done something to those dumb-ass kids? Christ, he don't have enough brains to zip his fly after he takes a leak."

"You don't need brains to hate or hurt somebody. Not when you own a couple of pit bulls."

"Ah, Jesus," Maxe said. "He wouldn't put them dogs on anybody."

"No? He threatened to put one on me this afternoon. And what if somebody else was around to goad him into doing it?

131

For instance, the fat bald guy who tried hassling me in the Eagle's Roost."

"Frank Hicks? He don't hang around with Ollie."

"Another Sentinel, though, right?"

"That's enough about the fuckin' Sentinels. That's enough, period." Maxe turned on his heel, changed his mind before he'd gone a step, and swung back to face me. "You keep it up with your questions, keep hassling people, you're gonna wind up damn sorry. I'm telling you, man."

"Who'll make me sorry? You?"

He answered that by hawking and spitting on the ground between us. Then he heeled around again, climbed into his pickup. The engine had been idling; he goosed the throttle until it roared, popped the clutch, and cut around in a tight turn that threw gravel and muddy water my way. I jumped back in time to keep most of it off me.

You're gonna wind up damn sorry. I'm telling you, man.

Well? It wasn't anything I hadn't already told myself.

14

I'd been right about Ralph Fassbinder: he didn't want any more to do with my unsubstantiated theories about the Sentinels and their involvement in the disappearances than he had with my earlier, nonspecific theories about the race angle. As soon as I started laying them out, in a booth in the bar section of Ron's Tavern & Grill, I could see him retreating, closing off. And by the time I was done talking, he wore his stony cop's face—the one they use on civilians they think have stepped over the line.

"I don't see it," he said flatly.

"What don't you see?"

"The connection you're trying to make."

"Pretty obvious, isn't it?"

"Is it?" He took a big swallow of his Sierra Nevada draft, licked away the foam clinging to his upper lip. "White woman and black man stumble into a town full of racists and get themselves blown away by a bloodthirsty mob. . . . Sounds like one of those crappy TV movies."

"I never said anything about a bloodthirsty mob."

"You might as well have," Fassbinder said. "You make Creekside sound like some backwoods Klan stronghold, where everybody runs around in sheets, burning crosses. It's just a village, like dozens of others up here, and most people who live there are law-abiding and no more bigoted than you or me. Sure, you'll find a few racists if you look hard enough, just like you'll find some anywhere else. But they aren't very damn likely to commit a racially motivated murder in their own backyard."

"Not unless they figured they could get away with it," I said. "Strength in numbers, Captain."

"Meaning the Sentinels."

"That's right. You didn't seem surprised when I mentioned the name."

"I wasn't. We've had reports."

"What kind of reports?"

"About that camp of theirs, their activities."

"And?"

"And what?" Fassbinder said. "The camp is on private property and they haven't broken a single law that we know about. They claim to be a religious organization, the camp a religious retreat. This is still a free country—they've got civil rights and First Amendment rights like everybody else."

"Funny how it's the people who want to deny others their civil and First Amendment rights who're always up front yammering about their own."

"No argument there. But the fact remains—"

"Yeah. What about this Colonel who runs the camp? You have an ID on him?"

"No. First I've heard of him. As far as we know, a man named Slingerland is head of the Sentinels. Reverend Dale Slingerland."

"Affiliated with the Christian National Emancipation League by any chance?"

Fassbinder nodded. "He's the nephew of Richard Chaffee. But that doesn't mean anything as far as the law is concerned. Chaffee isn't wanted for any offense—has no criminal record of any kind—and the same is true of the others in his league. Including Dale Slingerland."

"So they're all just a gaggle of Constitution-loving white supremacists."

"Like it or not," Fassbinder said, "that's right. Until we have proof to the contrary—"

"Who preach a doctrine of purifying America of what they call race-mixing and mongrelism. So naturally they wouldn't think there was anything wrong with an interracial couple loving up to each other smack in their midst, or ever even consider robbing a black man of his civil rights by killing him dead."

That bought me an even stonier look over the rim of his glass. "Proof," he said again slowly and distinctly. "You give me one piece of hard evidence, and my department—the federal boys too—will be all over the parties responsible like ants on a picnic lunch."

"One piece of hard evidence. I'll hold you to that."

"On the other hand," he said, "if you break any laws in my county, kick up the kind of trouble where somebody gets hurt, we'll be all over *you* like ants on a picnic lunch. Strike you as reasonable?"

"Sure," I said, just as tight and hard. "I have great respect for the law and for the rights of others. Victims' rights in particular."

"So do I. Whether you believe that or not."

We watched each other for a time. Fassbinder ended the staring contest by lifting his glass, draining it. "I've got to get home. Wife's expecting me." He slid out of the booth.

"I'll be in touch," I said.

"You do that. And you remember what I said."

After he was gone I sat brooding into my still-full glass. There was a simmer of anger in me, but none of it was directed at Fassbinder or the laws he was sworn to uphold; he was only doing his job the best way he knew how. It was anger at intolerance, persecution, tyranny—all the stupid concepts embraced by stupid individuals.

If those concepts and those types of people harmed Allison and Rob, I thought, they're not going to get away with it. Whatever it takes, whatever happens, I won't let them get away with it.

I ate a lonely dinner in the grill half of Ron's and then drove back to Creekside. It was nine-fifty by the dashboard clock when I swung off the highway and in along Main. A couple of dozen vehicles, mostly pickups and four-by-fours, jammed the street in the vicinity of the Eagle's Roost; jukebox noise and loud voices filtered out from the false-fronted tavern. Friday night in the boondocks. How many Sentinels, how many league members, were in there celebrating? I wondered. The thought made me feel even more cut off from my world, even more alone.

The Northern Comfort offered more loneliness—a dead-looking oasis in the wet night. I was still the only paying guest; the courtyard was deserted except for the Bartholomews' wreck, and no lights showed in any of the cabins. The light in the office window was a pale, cheerless rectangle blurred by rain that had slackened again to a fine, windblown drizzle.

The rear of the motel grounds, where number eleven waited, was ink-black outside the burrowing cones of my headlamps. When I stopped the car and shut the lights off, it was so dark I could barely make out the contours of the cabin a few feet away. The hair on my neck pulled a little, for no reason except that this kind of deep, almost subterranean black, in a place like Creekside, in a situation like the one I was up against here, combined to make me edgy and extra alert. Before I got out I mated my hand with the .38 in my coat pocket. And while I locked the car, exchanged the car keys for the door key and turned toward the cabin, I keened the night in that animallike way soldiers and lawmen learn from experience.

The excess caution accomplished two things: it allowed me to hear the two of them coming, even above the skirling, rattling sounds the wind made in the nearby evergreens, and it gave me just enough time to set myself against the attack. If they'd been professionals, I would not have heard them at all.

But they were amateurs, and in their haste and cowards' fear they made noise.

I swung around toward them, bracing my body against the cabin wall, trying to yank the .38 free; but there wasn't enough time for that, and just as well too, because in darkness and at close quarters the gun would not have done me any good. In the next second they were on me—black shapes, two of them, bulky, one with something upraised in his hand . . . grunting, one giving off a thin giggling laugh, the other spitting words like a snake's venom, "Teach you, you son of a bitch!" . . . both smelling of sweat and dry wool . . . jumbled impressions in the two or three heartbeats before it got wild and crazy. Then the one with the weapon swung at my head, and the rest of it seemed to happen at warp speed.

I ducked under the swing, kicked that one in the leg; he yelled and stumbled away from me. The second man hit me a glancing blow over the heart that didn't hurt much, didn't do any damage. I had my right hand out of the coat pocket by then, empty, and I jabbed at him and missed and jabbed again; my knuckles struck bone and the shock of impact was like an eruption in my armpit. But it didn't hurt him either. He grunted, swore, tried to drive his knee into my crotch. He didn't have enough leverage, but I did; when his knee came up I turned my body and side-kicked his other shin. The blow was solid enough to stagger him. I managed to smack him some-where in the face with my fist, another solid connection that knocked him down, mewling like a cat.

The first man came charging back hard and fast. Whatever he was swinging caught me on the left shoulder and the arm im-mediately went numb. He pulled back to club me again; I had just enough time to twist my head and body out of the way. The damn thing made a noise like a thunderclap when it smashed into the wall above and behind me. His arm was up where I could see it; I got a grip on the woolen sleeve of his coat and yanked the arm down hard, at the same time bringing a knee up to meet it. I heard and felt his wrist break. Heard him scream with the pain, heard the club clatter on the wet ground.

I shoved him away, scraped rain out of my face so I could look for the second one. But he'd had enough of me. For a few seconds I saw the shape of him—getting to his feet, swaying like a sapling in the wind—and then he merged with the blackness and I was listening to the pound of his shoes on the gravel, running away.

The one with the broken wrist yelled in a high-pitched voice, "You dirty bastard, you *fuck,* I'll get you for this!" I yelled back at him, "Come on, then, come on come on," but he was all through too. He lurched away, fell, scrambled up, and was gone.

Like a damn fool I gave chase, my numb left arm flopping uselessly. I fumbled the .38 out, and in those first few rage-fueled seconds I would have used it if I'd had a target to shoot at. But all I had was darkness and a confused clutter of sounds. The ground underfoot was flat and carpeted with pine needles; otherwise I wouldn't have gotten as far as I did—twenty or thirty yards—before I tripped over something, sprawled head-long.

Automatically I threw my right arm out to break the fall, and when I landed, hard and jarring, the gun went off. No damage, bullet into the ground, but the recoil and the flat, too-loud re-port broke the wildness in me, kick-started the rational part of my brain. *Stupid. Stupid, stupid.* I hauled back on my knees, struggling to hear something over the wheezing plaint of my breathing. Rushing gurgle of water: the creek must be close by. But that and the wind were all I could make out.

It was over. For now.

Lucky, I thought as I staggered back toward the cabin. Lucky I hadn't fallen on the gun when it went off. Lucky I wasn't lying on the ground in front of the cabin with a busted head. Lucky the two sluggers had gotten away into the night before I could shoot one of them.

I found the car first and leaned against it with my face upturned, sucking at the moist air. My chest felt tight, hot. The hissing blood-pound in my ears was like surf in a storm.

Distantly a car engine roared to life and tires bit squealing into pavement. So long, you bastards, I thought. If you're thinking about coming back later with reinforcements, you'll wish you hadn't.

Some feeling began to return to my left arm, a hot tingling that put a throb in my fingertips. Pretty soon I could move it all right, hands and fingers too; nothing broken. I fished out my car keys, unlocked the driver's door. The other item I keep clipped under the dash is a six-cell flashlight; I yanked it free, leaned back out, and relocked the door. I had lost the cabin key sometime during the skirmish and it wasn't likely I could find it unaided in the dark.

Even with the torch, it took me almost five minutes to locate the key: it was half hidden in a puddle. I also identified the thing the one slugger had tried to brain me with—a three-foot length of stove wood. The rain had quickened again and the wind had gone gusty; the storm's racket shut out all other sounds. But there had been plenty of noise in the past few minutes; and plenty of shifting arrows of light from my flash. Yet neither of the Bartholomews had put in an appearance. Whatever they'd seen or heard, they hadn't wanted any part of it or its aftermath. Mrs. Bartholomew: *Lord's business, not mine.* Yeah.

Shivering, I keyed open the cabin door. Warm enough inside but I turned the space heater up anyway, as high as it would go. I locked the door, wedged the only chair under the knob. I was on my way into the tiny bathroom for a damage check, when reaction set in.

Dizziness, nausea, a flare of pain in my shoulder that radiated up into my neck. I sat on the bed with my head down between my knees, breathing slowly, waiting for it all to ease. I'd been through this before, too many times, and I knew it wouldn't take long. Four or five minutes this time before I felt steady enough to get back on my feet. And once I was upright I was all right again, except for a shaky feeling that would linger awhile longer.

The fight damage wasn't bad. Scrape on my neck, gathering bruise on my shoulder, a painful swelling on one knuckle. But my topcoat was ruined: rip in the sleeve and another application of ground-in mud that would never come out. I stood under a hot shower for a few minutes to treat the shoulder soreness. When I came out I put on my robe and moved the chair under the window and sat there looking out past the edge of the shade, the .38 on the table next to me.

I sat for a long time, nursing my anger, drawing energy from it. They didn't come back. Nobody drove into the lot, nobody came out of the office building—nothing at all happened.

The reason for the ambush was clear enough: I was getting too close to the corruption that lay beneath the surface of Creekside, too close to the truth about Allison and Rob. That giggling laugh from the one whose wrist I'd snapped . . . Ollie Ballard, no mistake. I'd pushed him too far this afternoon and he'd come shoving back with a vengeance. The other one could have been anybody; his voice had been robbed of familiarity by the wind and my own adrenaline rush. One thing sure: whoever the second man was, he, like Ballard, was a badge-carrying member of the Sentinels.

Had the Colonel or one of his underlings ordered the ambush?

No. Trying to bust somebody's head in a two-man sneak attack is an amateur's ploy, not a paramilitary one. If the Sentinels had already murdered two people, they wouldn't hesitate to murder a third to protect themselves; and if they wanted me out of the way, they'd have sent trained soldiers to do it with guns or knives, not a couple of lowlifes armed with stove wood.

Ballard and his partner acting on their own hook, then. But it wouldn't have been Ballard's idea; he wasn't smart enough to have an idea. A follower, not a leader. The other one was behind the attack, conception and set-up both.

You don't want to fuck with me. I'll rip your face off.

Frank Hicks?

You're gonna wind up damn sorry.

Art Maxe?

No use speculating. I didn't know enough about either of them, or enough yet about anyone connected with the Sentinels or the Christian National Emancipation League.

At midnight, fatigue drove me out of the chair and into bed. The .38 went too; I kept it close beside me like a cold, waiting lover. I was asleep in a minute or two, but it wasn't a good sleep. I kept waking up every half hour or so, hearing things, imagining more menace that wasn't there. By the time gray dawn crept in around the window shade, I'd slept a total of maybe four hours, none of it deep or restful, and I knew I was all through for this night.

The anger was still with me. Hot and hurting and hungry this morning, like something waiting to be fed.

15

The rain had quit by the time I came out at seven-fifteen, wearing my torn and mud-caked topcoat with the .38 tucked again into the pocket. But it was only a lull; the cloud cover was still low and restless and veined with black, and the cold air still had that moist ozone smell. There was wood smoke in the air too—gobs of it pulsing out of the chimney at the rear of the office building.

Under a lean-to arrangement tacked onto the rear wall over there, Ed Bartholomew stood hunched and plucking three-foot lengths of stove wood from a winter stack. Source of the chunk Ballard had used last night, maybe. I detoured that way, walking slow in deference to the aches and pains I would have to live with that day. My left shoulder was so stiff I couldn't lift the arm over my head. The knuckle on my right hand throbbed too, but the swelling had gone down during the night; bruised, not broken, as I'd feared at first. It wouldn't hamper me much if I needed to use the gun.

Bartholomew straightened as I approached, turned with an armload of wood. His movements were as slow and painful as mine, from whatever joint or vertebra problems plagued him. When he saw me he stopped and stood stiffly, his back bowed, waiting.

"Morning," I said.

"Morning. You checking out?"

"No. I'll be here awhile longer."

"How much longer?"

"I can't say. Depends on how fast things come together."

"What things?"

"What things do you think, Mr. Bartholomew?"

He wouldn't hold my eyes. He said, "Your business, none of mine," and started to turn away.

I was tired of hearing that cop-out phrase; it stirred my anger. I stopped him again by saying, "Quite a commotion last night."

"Commotion?"

"Over by my cabin. Around nine-thirty."

"That so?"

"Didn't hear the noise? Some of it was pretty loud."

"Didn't hear a thing," Bartholomew said. "Missus and me was watching a program. She don't hear too good—had the sound turned way up."

"Sure you did."

"I got to take this wood inside," he said.

I let him get as far as the door this time. "Don't you care what the commotion was about?"

"No," he said without looking at me.

"Happened on your property. For all you know, it could've been bad trouble and I'm thinking of suing you."

"Can't get blood from a turnip. All me and Ruth's got is each other and the Lord God almighty." And then he was gone inside. I heard the lock click as soon as the door shut behind him.

The car started slow and balky this morning, the same as its owner, and the engine made knocking noises until it warmed up. I'd put a lot of miles on it lately, well over a hundred thousand in all the years I'd had it. Good car, but if I was going to keep it much longer, I'd have to have the engine completely overhauled. Maybe it was time to buy another set of wheels. Kerry thought it was—"something newer, with a little more pizzazz." Newer, possibly, but pizzazz was for younger guys with image needs and psychological attachments to speed and sleek-and-shiny hunks of metal. Old farts like me didn't need to bond with the thing we drove from point A to point B. All I cared about was that the hunk of metal could be depended upon to make each trip without adding any more hassles to my already disordered life.

I drove down to the general store, which wasn't open yet, and spent another three-plus minutes inside my least-favorite public phone shell. As early as it was, Joe DeFalco's home number was busy. Busy speeding along the information highway, I hoped. I paged through a damp Lassen County directory, to find out if there was a listing for George Duquesne. No listing. Then I tried DeFalco's number a second time, with the same results. Busy, busy. Just like I was going to be.

I left the car where it was and went by shank's mare to the Modoc Cafe. Half a dozen unfamiliar customers and Lorraine on duty. The buzz of conversation died when I walked in; eyes watched me until I looked their way, then pretended I was a larger version of Yehudi, the little man who wasn't there. I ordered coffee and tried to ask Lorraine about George Duquesne. She wouldn't talk to me or even look at me. I was about to try the question on the customers—in a loud voice, all of them at once—when the door opened and the blond kid, Johnny, walked in alone.

He was three paces inside when he spotted me. His about-face was sudden and sharp enough to have pleased an army drill instructor. I went after him as fast as I could move. Just fast enough: I caught up with him, laid a hard hand on his shoulder in front of Trilby's Hardware & Electric.

"Hold on, Johnny. What's your hurry?"

For a tight little clutch of seconds I thought he might shake me off, run away as he had yesterday. Scared, all right, but not a coward; there was at least some courage in him. He even held my eyes when he finally turned.

"I told you," he said, "I don't want to talk to you. Not about . . . you know."

I studied his face. Same as yesterday, only cleaner. Not much chance that Johnny had been the second slugger last night, but I was looking close at every male I encountered today—Bartholomew, the Modoc's customers, Johnny. I had not only broken

Ollie Ballard's wrist, I'd gotten in a few good licks on his partner, enough to mark him.

"I'm not going to push you on that subject, Johnny. I just want to ask you one question."

"Yeah? What question?"

"George Duquesne. Can you—"

"Oh, Jesus!"

"Take it easy. All I want to know is how to get to his ranch."

Blink. "His ranch?"

"You know where it is, don't you?"

". . . Yeah, I guess."

"Directions, okay? Then I'll leave you alone."

"Why don't you go away and leave everybody alone?"

"Can't do that, and you know why. Duquesne's ranch?"

He hesitated again, but not for long. "South on the highway about three miles. You'll see a sign for Parson's Flat. You go out there—another couple of miles." Blink. "But it won't do you no good."

"Going out to the ranch? Why not?"

"Duquesne, he don't let nobody in."

"Strangers, you mean?"

"Not anybody. He don't like people. He's a recluse." He pronounced it "reek-loose."

"Well, maybe he'll make an exception in my case."

"I don't think so," the kid said. Then, in a rush, "You better watch out, mister."

"For what? Duquesne?"

"You just better watch out, that's all."

Cryptic warnings. Creekside was as full of them as it was of pretense, denial, and outright lies.

Johnny was right about the Duquesne ranch. The drive out there was a waste of time.

I found the place easily enough—a sprawling little enclave of more than a dozen buildings of varying sizes, tucked away behind chain-link fencing. All the buildings were painted a gleaming white. An electronic gate barred entrance to the property. The look of the gate and the absence of barbed wire made me wonder if the fence might be electrified.

On one of the support pillars was an intercom thing; I used it and a male voice answered, probably at the main house. When I gave my name and asked to see Duquesne on an urgent matter, there was a short silence while he either conferred with somebody or checked a list to see if my name was on it. The voice said then that it was sorry, Mr. Duquesne was not available. How about if I made an appointment for later? I said. No appointments, he said. I told him the urgent matter had to do with the Sentinels, but that didn't buy me anything either. The voice informed me in chillier tones that Mr. Duquesne was not available to anyone at any time for any reason, and cut me off before I could make another pitch.

Back into the car, back out to the highway, but not back to Creekside—not yet. I drove south another few miles, to the next little village, and ate a quick breakfast at a cafe there. The restaurant had a public phone; this time DeFalco's line was clear and he answered right away.

"About time," he said. He sounded revved up; I could almost hear him licking his chops. Sure. For him all of this was armchair intrigue and another phantom shot at a Pulitzer. "Everything okay up there?"

"Depends on what you mean by okay."

"You. I meant with you."

The anger in me had quieted to a stubborn resolve, and I didn't want to heat it up again by going into a rehash of last night's trouble. I said, "I'm hanging in. I slept with my gun."

"Freudian," he said. "Does Kerry know about this?"

"No, and you'd better not tell her."

"You talk to the Lassen sheriff's man?"

"Briefly." I filled him in on my nonproductive discussion with Fassbinder.

147

"Well, he's not the only one up there with a closed mind. I called the editor of the *North Corner Gazette* last night—that's a biweekly in Susanville—and asked some pointed questions about hate crimes in his bailiwick. He admitted to hearing whispers about both the Sentinels and the Christian National Emancipation League, but said he couldn't pin them down."

"He must not have tried very hard."

"He didn't. He's an old-timer—ambition all dried up, disinclined to open up a cesspool in his own backyard. The old ostrich crap."

"Lot of that going around these days."

"Yeah. But he did tell me one thing that ties in. There've been a batch of incidents in the Corner in recent months that can be classified only as hate crimes."

"Interesting."

"I take it Fassbinder didn't mention them."

"Not a peep. Too inflammatory, I suppose. What kind of incidents, Joe?"

"Vandalism at a Vietnamese restaurant in Alturas, more of the same at the home of a black family near the Oregon border, hate mail sent to about a dozen black, Asian, and Jewish families in Lassen and Modoc counties. No overt violence—not so far. You can smell it coming, though."

"The Sentinels," I said, "sure as hell."

"Yeah, but there's no evidence it's an organized campaign or who's behind it. According to the editor, the local authorities have it pegged as random stuff, nothing serious."

"Fassbinder claims he has no idea who the Colonel is. You get a line on the man?"

"Damn right," DeFalco said. "If the ID is right, and I think it is, he's a hell of a big fish."

"Big how?"

"Wanted by the FBI and ATF for masterminding the theft of a truckload of weapons from a federal armory in Missouri a couple of years ago. There's also a Tennessee state fugitive warrant on him—suspicion of conspiracy to commit murder."

"White supremacist ties?"

"Oh, hell yes. His name is Darnell, Colonel Benjamin Darnell. Ex-Vietnam vet, ex-mercenary soldier in Nicaragua and half a dozen small African nations. Thrown out of the U.S. Army for conduct unbecoming an officer . . . racially motivated assault on a black noncom. Reputed to've spent some time at Butler's Aryan Nations hideaway as a training officer. And here's the clincher: his brother-in-law is cut from the same lousy cloth—linked to a couple of Arizona-based racist groups and guess which one of the same in California."

"The Christian National Emancipation League."

"Right."

"Did the name Slingerland come up in connection with Darnell? Reverend Dale Slingerland?"

"Richard Chaffee's nephew. No direct link to Darnell, but Slingerland and the Colonel's brother-in-law helped form a militia outfit in northern Arizona a couple of years ago. Is Slingerland mixed up with the Sentinels too?"

"According to Fassbinder, he's the one running the camp."

"Christ, that place is a real nest. But you figure Darnell's the one in charge?"

"From all indications. Does Darnell's description match the one I gave you?"

"Right down to the hawk nose."

"Question now," I said, "is whether or not he's still at the camp. When I had my little run-in with his Jeep the other night, he was headed out to the highway. Could've been a short trip, or it could've been a long one—to another nest, maybe."

"Can you find out one way or the other?"

"I can try."

"Okay, good. Any luck with that rancher Duquesne?"

"I went out to his ranch this morning, but I couldn't get in. Whole place is fenced like a fortress."

"No surprise. I'll lay odds he's one of them too. Hard-core right-winger, worth a couple of million bucks. Used to be active in ultraconservative politics in the Corner."

"Used to be?"

"He dropped out about five years ago. Reclusive since then—very low-profile."

"Well, that's easy enough to explain. Racist all along, went the hard-line route five years ago and got hooked up with Chaffee and Darnell."

"Reads that way to me too."

"Anything else, Joe?"

"That's the package for now," he said. "Doesn't look too good for those missing kids, does it?"

"Let's stay off that. I'm stressed enough as it is."

"Sure. Sorry. What's your next move?"

"Try to get a line on Darnell's whereabouts—some hard evidence for the feds, if not the county law."

"How?"

"My lookout. You just keep riding the information highway."

"Will do. But call me later, whether you find out anything or not. Don't leave me hanging and sweating."

"I won't," I said. As long as I wasn't hanging and sweating somewhere myself.

A thin drizzle was starting again as I drove up Lodgepole Lane, on the hill above Creekside. Through the wedges cleared by the clacking wipers I could see somebody moving around in the cluttered side yard of Cermak's Bargains. A stake-bed truck had been backed up to one of the lean-tos and somebody bundled in a coat with a hood like a monk's cowl seemed to be struggling to lift a large, round, heavy object into the bed.

The gate in the crazy-quilt fence stood open; I parked in front of it and walked along the drive and over to the truck. Mike Cermak's bearded face peered at me unhappily from inside the coat hood. He quit wrestling with the heavy object—an old, rusty water heater—and nervously slapped gloved hands against his side, as I approached.

"You again."

"Me again. Want some help with that heater?"

"No." But then he changed his mind and said, "Yeah, all right. Fucking thing weighs a ton."

I got a grip on the lower end of it and together we muscled it into the truck. Cermak climbed up after it and began to rope it down.

"So what do you want this time, man?" he asked while he worked. He sounded wearily resigned—the tone of a man who has done something against his better judgment and who is certain he will regret it for the rest of his life.

"Yesterday you said something about a badge. When you took the load of supplies to the Sentinels' camp, they gave you a badge to show at the gate."

"Before I went. Guy who came here with the order gave it to me. Nobody gets in without one."

"What kind of badge?"

"Blue and white triangle, made out of felt."

"Just show it to the guard on the gate?"

"And wore it the whole time I was inside. Pinned to my shirt."

"They take it back when you left?"

"No. Guard was supposed to, maybe, but he didn't."

"What'd you do with it? Keep it or throw it away?"

"Shit, man, I should've burned it."

"But you didn't. So you still have it."

"Yeah. Figured I might need it again if they bought any more of my stuff. But they never came around again."

"How about if I buy the badge from you?"

"Buy it? You serious?"

"Don't I sound serious?"

"Crazy if you go out there by yourself . . ."

"I don't want to argue or haggle, Mike." I got my wallet out, showed him a pair of tens from inside. "Twenty dollars, take it or leave it."

He looked at the money with a kind of thin contempt—not

so much for the bills as for himself for coveting the filthy stuff. Then he tied one last knot in the rope, tested his handiwork, and jumped down. "Wait here," he said.

He went away into the house. In five minutes he was back with the badge, holding it between thumb and forefinger as if it were something he didn't like touching even with gloves on. Blue-bordered isosceles triangle about four inches in diameter, the felt thin and cheap; the word *Beware* was stitched in blue thread at an up-slanted angle in the white center. A closed safety pin was hooked through one point of the triangle. Professionally done and crude at the same time. Badge of evil.

I held the two tens out, but Cermak wouldn't take them. "Keep your money," he said. "I don't need it that bad."

"You sure? You took their money."

"I didn't know who they were then."

"You'd have taken more of it later if they'd come back. That's why you kept the badge, isn't it?"

"Told myself it was. But if they had come back . . . hell, man, I don't know. If I'd been stoned enough, could be I'd've told them to shove their business up their Nazi poop-chutes." He grinned self-mockingly. "If I'd been stoned enough."

I put the money and my wallet away, hid the badge inside my coat pocket. Then, on impulse, I made a V with my right index and middle fingers. "Peace, huh?"

"Oh, yeah," he said. "Power to the people."

16

Timberline Road was backcountry, all right. Deep backcountry.

"Seven, eight miles west of Creekside," Mike Cermak had said. But the route you had to travel to get there was so circuitous, the distance seemed twice as long. Cermak's directions weren't too good either; I made a pair of wrong turns, and managed to get back on the right track mostly by accident. The weather made the hunt even more difficult. The drizzle continued in a thin, straight-downward fall—there was almost no wind—and an undulant mist obscured the hilly terrain, filled every hollow as if with mounds of half-frozen smoke. Altogether I spent an hour on a network of rough, narrow lanes before I finally passed a signpost that informed me I had somehow blundered onto Timberline Road. Another sign alongside it proclaimed NOT A THROUGH ROAD.

I hadn't seen a building in several miles, nor a driveway or branch lane that might lead to a hidden farm or ranch. Just thick stands of pine and Douglas fir, their needled branches leaking moisture, the stands broken now and then by rock-strewn meadows and hillsides patched with second-growth timber and notched with deadfalls. Old logging area, I thought; old logging road. Empty wilderness now, remote—just the right kind of terrain for a paramilitary outpost.

I followed Timberline Road for nearly a mile, through dips and curves and several switchbacks. Down and up and back down again. The road surface kept worsening, until it was so

153

heavily pocked that I had to slow to thirty in order to maneuver around the worst of the chucks. I rolled through yet another tight turn, and fifty yards beyond, the road came to an abrupt end. Or, rather, free access came to an abrupt end.

A semaphore lift gate, like the ones you see at railroad crossings, had been erected to bar the way. Alongside it at the edge of the road was a military-style sentry box. Two signs were mounted on the gate—a big red stop sign, and one that had been semiprofessionally painted in heavy black letters:

PRIVATE PROPERTY
NO ENTRANCE WITHOUT PERMISSION
WHITE CHRISTIANS ONLY!

I stopped the car, sat there for a minute or so with the engine running and the wipers slapping away. Past the lift gate, trees had been cleared to open up a fifty-yard-wide section of meadowland; a long, high chain-link fence ran through the middle of the cleared area, with another gate in it double-barring the road. The fence and the second gate were topped with strands of wicked-looking barbed wire. The overall effect was of a military no-man's land, of the sort that used to exist along the border between West and East Germany.

There was nobody inside the sentry box, nobody in sight on either side of the chain-link fence. Beyond the fence, the road was visible for another seventy-five yards—resurfaced asphalt in there—before it vanished into a thick copse of Douglas fir. The buildings that formed the compound were well hidden behind the trees and the drear gray wall of rain and mist.

So where's the guard? I thought.

Off taking a leak, maybe.

Well?

I shifted position on the seat. The movement made me aware of the weight of the gun in my coat pocket. I hauled the thing out, held it for a few seconds, then snapped it into the metal clips under the dash. I was one man and there were God knew how many wackos with God knew how much firepower somewhere close by. It was enough of a risk just trying to get myself in there; carrying heat on the Sentinels' turf was begging for the kind of trouble I could neither handle nor afford.

I shut the car down, slid out. There was a little wind here, dead-cold; it blew rain into my face, and I could hear it making empty muttering sounds in the trees. Nothing else to hear. And still nothing to see as I crossed to the lift bar. As I stepped over it, I glanced inside the sentry box. Box was exactly what it was: an upright wooden coffin, just large enough for one man, containing a bench and nothing else.

The gate in the fence, I saw as I neared it, would open electronically—by means of a remote control unit in the guard's possession, no doubt. The strands of barbed wire and the amount of fencing argued against electrification. As threatening as the coils of wire were, a man could climb up and over without ripping himself too badly—even a man my age—but he'd make a damn fine target while he was doing it. Nobody with any sense would try to get in or out of the camp that way.

I wondered if the fence ran all the way around it. Probably not; a compound as large as the one Cermak had indicated would require a prohibitive amount of chain-link fencing to completely enclose it. They'd only fence the more open areas, I thought. There would be ways to get in and out through the denser patches of forest, but you'd need to be a wilderness tracker to find them without getting yourself lost.

I turned away from the fence. And I wasn't alone any longer. A guy was running toward me from the trees on the left, in a crouched posture and with the stealth of a commando. The hackles lifted on my neck. He looked like a commando too: camouflage jacket, plain fatigue trousers, heavy black army boots, walkie-talkie clipped to his belt, soldier's cap worn backward the way the Colonel's Jeep driver had worn his, as if in some kind of protest against standard military procedure; and clutched in both hands, the muzzle tilted up in front of his body, a semiautomatic assault rifle with a clip that looked a foot long. The weapon wasn't aimed straight at me because it didn't need to be. He could spray enough bullets with that thing to cut down a dozen men in a matter of seconds.

I walked forward slowly to meet him, my hands down at my sides and my spine and posture stiff. I had a crawly feeling of other eyes on me, eyes and more weapons, but it was a reaction to the surroundings, the sudden heightening of tension. They would not have stationed more than one man out there. Others patrolling inside the compound, sure. But more than one guard to open and close the gates, when they had no cause to expect trouble, was a waste of limited manpower.

Just this one and me, then. For now.

He stopped moving when he was on the road and some ten feet separated us. He growled at me, "What the hell you want here, mister?"

Instead of answering, I halved the distance between us, to send a message—only about half true—that I wasn't afraid of him. He was young, no more than voting age, if that; fair-complected and ice-eyed. Pure Aryan storm trooper, I thought. Adolf the house painter would have loved him.

He didn't like what he was seeing any more than I did. His face pinched up and an ugliness came into his eyes. I'm an olive-skinned Italian, and he'd been conditioned to hate anybody with skin darker than his own. I told myself I wasn't dark enough to make him positive of my ancestry, that he'd be too disciplined to act on impulse, that I was smarter and more experienced and I could bluff him all right if I held on to my cool. But how could you be sure of anything when you were up against a gun-bearing white supremacist?

"What you want here?" he said again. Hard, clipped, but with an edge of nervousness that could be bad or good, depending on how well I worked him.

I showed him a flat, cold stare of my own. If there was one thing a kid like him would respond to, it was authority—the tougher the better. "Put that weapon up, soldier. You don't deserve to carry it."

". . . What?"

"You heard me. Why weren't you at your post?"

It was six or seven ticks before he said, "I don't know you, mister. I don't have to answer to you."

"Then you'll answer to the Colonel."

"The Colonel? Listen—"

"No, *you* listen. You deserted your post. Either give me a satisfactory explanation or I'll put your sorry ass on report."

He ran his tongue along the underside of his upper lip. "I don't know you," he said again, not quite as hard this time. "You look like a dago . . ."

"Is that right? Say it once more."

"I don't—"

"Call me a dago once more."

"I didn't call you a dago, I said you looked—"

"My name is Anderson," I said. "You hear me, you little shit? *Anderson.* I served with Colonel Darnell in Vietnam, in Africa. I trained with him at Hayden Lake. I'm here at his request, soldier, you got that? The Colonel's request!"

I thought I had him now—maybe. Uncertainty in his eyes, the beginnings of anxiety. He *had* been away from his post; and if there was one man he feared, it would be Colonel Benjamin Darnell, whether Darnell was presently in the camp or not.

He did the lip-tonguing thing again. After which he said, "Your badge?" I saw the word "sir" start to form, but he wasn't quite ready to go that far yet.

"Right here." I fished the blue and white triangle out of my pocket, held it up for him to see. "Well?"

It was the convincer. "I'm sorry, Mr. Anderson," he said in a softer, backing-down voice, "but you weren't supposed to leave your vehicle—"

"I was looking for you, soldier. Now answer my question: Why'd you desert your post?"

"I . . . had to relieve myself."

Right. "That's no excuse. Why didn't you piss behind the sentry box?"

"I don't know . . . I guess I needed to stretch my legs . . ."

"Get over there and open those gates. I'm late enough as it is."

One more obstacle: the walkie-talkie. If he decided to check inside before letting me pass . . . but he didn't. He said, "Yes, sir," and went to work the lift bar. As I'd figured, he used a remote device to open the gate in the fence.

I walked around him to the car, pinning the badge to the front of my jacket, then drove ahead to where he stood more or less at attention and stopped and slid the window down. "Don't leave your post again, soldier. For any reason. Understood?"

"Yes, sir. You won't report me to the Colonel?"

I just looked at him. Let him stew in his own sour juices.

"I'm . . . I shouldn't have said you looked like a dago. You don't, Mr. Anderson, not really . . ."

Christ. Vicious on the one hand, pathetic on the other. Stupid little boy who didn't know how to be a man, playing a deadly man's game. I ran the window up and left him standing there, clutching his rifle in the rain.

So now I was in. Fine, rum dandy. All I had to do was get back out again in one piece.

Well, I didn't need much time to accomplish my mission. I had that in my favor, and I also had some leverage if I needed it: Cermak knew I'd gone out there and I could claim that DeFalco knew it too, and the Sentinels and Colonel Benjamin Darnell in particular couldn't afford the kind of heat my sudden disappearance would bring. I'd be all right. Sure, I would.

Sure . . .

The nest itself was half again as large as Cermak had led me to believe—and chillingly impressive when you came out of the trees and saw it all at once. There were a couple of dozen

buildings scattered around ten or twelve acres of treeless terrain, about half of them prefabs and the rest made of un-
trimmed logs and slab wood. The largest, about the size of a
small gymnasium, stood by itself off on the right. Meeting hall, I
thought, and the annex on one side a kind of administration
building. The windows in both were short and narrow, like
embrasures; that would be where they'd figure to fort up during a siege. The annex would also be where the Colonel and
Dale Slingerland had their offices and planning rooms. A place
for me to avoid.

Light brightened the windows in the annex, those in several
of the other buildings. Electric light, supplied by heavy-duty
portable generators; I hadn't seen any power poles along
Timberline Road and I doubted the county would have strung
lines anywhere close enough for them to tap into. No water or
sewer facilities out here either, which meant wells or cisterns,
privies or chemical toilets. Primitive. But nonetheless efficient.
U.S. soldiers in war-zone camps had had to make do with a hell
of a lot less.

Directly ahead was a rectangular, mud-churned parade
ground the length and width of a football field. It lay empty
now, and the rain and the ripped-up surface gave it a bleak
aspect—a surrealistic battleground after the dead and wounded
had been removed, the surreality provided by the row of Porta
Potties squatting at the far end. The weather was another point
in my favor. I could see sporadic activity, people and vehicles
moving here and there, but most of the camp's occupants were
busy indoors, where it was warm and dry and I wouldn't attract
their attention.

At the parade ground the road forked into two branches that
I thought would circle the compound and then rejoin. It would
also connect with a second exit road somewhere at the rear. A
man like Darnell, with his military background, would not per-
mit a camp like this to be built without more than one way in
and out, particularly with the Timberline Road route passing
through Creekside before the highway could be reached. The

second road would be an escape route, connecting with other backcountry roads and then the highway at some uninhabited location farther south. Probably little used except when they were bringing in large shipments of goods that might snag someone's attention. Illegal weapons, for instance.

I followed the left fork, past three long, low structures that had the look of barracks. Unpaved lanes branched off at intervals, giving access to the various buildings and creating a loose grid pattern. I saw small individual cabins, a recreation field complete with a baseball backstop, two large windowless buildings that might have been warehouses, and then—in a way the most disturbing of all the components in this odious little enclave—a rough log church with a cross jutting high above its entrance. The cross was plain, unpainted, and there was nothing religious about it laid up there against the gray sky. It looked exactly like one of the crosses men in sheets and hoods would douse with kerosene and set on fire.

Beyond the church, as the road began its loop around to the rear of the camp, I jounced past a big open garage and motor pool. At least a dozen vehicles—Jeeps, military surplus trucks, vans with smoke-tinted windows, three nondescript passenger cars—were visible inside and outside the garage. The passenger cars were a small relief; mine blended right in with them. None of the three men working the motor pool paid me the slightest attention.

I spotted the escape road easily enough—wide and graveled, angling away into the trees. On the far side of where it branched off, another windowless building squatted like an islet in a sea of trampled grass and mud. It was too small to be another supply warehouse. But it had a set of wide double doors, and next to them a normal-sized door. All three doors were shut and there was nobody around outside that I could see.

Armory, I thought. Has to be.

Now or never. I'd gone far enough anyway; I could see the

meeting hall and annex from there and I didn't want to drive past it, or to get within recognition distance of it.

There were no other vehicles on the road in either direction. I made a tight U-turn, parked on the near side of the escape road, then walked back across to the motor pool. One of the mechanics was outside, well apart from the other two, doing something inside a canvas-topped Jeep. I went straight to him, putting on a hard face as I walked like an actor getting into character.

The guy was hunched over under the Jeep's wheel, probably working on the ignition system. I stopped by the open door and said, "Question for you, soldier."

He twisted his head to look up at me. Thirtyish, heavy beard stubble flecking his cheeks, brown eyes that didn't have much going on behind them. Another pea-brain. A frown began to reshape his mouth; they'd all know each other here, and he didn't know me.

"Yeah?"

"New in camp," I said. "Just got in. You seen the Colonel?"

He glanced at the badge pinned to my jacket, and the frown smoothed away. If he'd said the Colonel wasn't in the compound, I had an answer ready to allay any more suspicions he might have. But that wasn't what he said.

"Not since this morning. You been to his office?"

"Yeah. He's supposed to be at the armory."

"Not there, huh?"

"Not there."

"Who's on watch? Matt?"

"He didn't tell me his name."

"What'd he say about the Colonel?"

I shrugged. "He didn't know either of us would be there."

"Somebody screwed up then. What're you? Another ordnance man?"

"Supplier," I said. "Fresh shipment coming in."

"What we got this time?"

"What do you need most?"

"Hell, I dunno. AK-47s?" As if he were asking me.

"That's what you're getting."

"Good. Man, that's good."

"What else you got in there? Plenty of everything?"

"Sure, plenty. Didn't Matt show you?"

"No. Waiting on the Colonel."

"Well, you go on back over. Colonel's supposed to meet you, he'll show up before long."

I nodded and returned to the road. Two choices: keep going to the car and out of here, or a quick check of the armory first. I knew for sure now that Darnell was still holed up in the camp—one piece of hard evidence for the feds. I knew there was a weapons stash too, but what I didn't have was a clear idea of how extensive it was. I hadn't wanted to risk pressing the mechanic, but it was possible I could fast-talk the guard named Matt. The more definite the information I had to pass along . . .

Decision made: I was already past the car. I quit the road and slogged at an angle through the grass and mud to the normal-sized door in the armory wall. When I rapped on the panel I got no response. I tried the knob; it turned under my hand. So I pushed the door inward, stuck my head inside.

Office cubicle, empty except for a steel desk and a couple of folding chairs. On the left was a partially ajar inner door; through the opening I could see a small section of floor space brightly lighted by overhead fluorescents. I listened, didn't hear anything, and went all the way into the office, leaving the outer door open. When I pushed on the inner door it made a faint creaking sound; I took my hand away. The opening, now, was just wide enough for my head and shoulders.

Christ.

The building must have been a hundred feet long by sixty wide, with a twelve-foot ceiling, and ninety percent of the floor space was taken up with crates and boxes stacked high. A few of the crates were huge: mortars and mortar shells. Short, squat boxes: handguns of different calibers and assorted ammunition.

Oblong wooden crates: assault rifles, automatic weapons. Enough firepower to start a small and bloody war.

Across from where I stood was a cluster of gray metal cases, one of which had been opened and the top left off; excelsior dribbled out over the near side. I stayed put for a few seconds, listening to the wind and rain. Then I walked over quick and soft for a look inside the box.

Fragmentation grenades. Government issue. The side of the case was stamped with the words U.S. ARMY—

"Hey, you there! What the fuck you think you're doing?"

17

The voice was harsh, edged with violence; it bunched the flesh between my shoulder blades, created a feeling of constriction across the top of my skull. I turned in slow segments, with my hands in plain sight. He stood a dozen feet away, legs slightly bent and both arms extended—a shooter's stance. A military-issue .45 automatic was this one's weapon of choice, and it was aimed straight at my belt buckle.

The inside of my mouth had gone dry, but I did not want him to see me working up spit to moisten it. Just as well, because when I spoke through the dryness, my voice came out sounding as harsh as his.

"Banged on the door but nobody answered, so I walked in. Where were you?"

He ignored that. He'd come out from behind a pile of ammunition boxes opposite. "Don't you know no better than to come waltzing in here without permission?"

"Nobody told me. I just got into camp a little while ago. Your name Matt?"

"What if it is? How'd you know that?"

"How do you think? The Colonel sent me over."

No reaction. His eyes were all over me, missing nothing including the badge, but the suspicion in them didn't go away. He was about thirty, fair-haired like the one out at the main gate, built like a pro halfback. He wore olive drab fatigues, the blouse short-sleeved in spite of the weather; knots of muscle were visible along his forearms and upper arms. But the worst thing was, his eyes and face displayed more intelligence than the other Sentinels I'd encountered.

"What's your name?" he demanded.

"Anderson."

"Why'd the Colonel send you over?"

"See what you got stockpiled. I put together a shipment of AK-47s for him, and I can lay hands on plenty of other ordnance where they came from—Browning machine pistols, M79 grenade launchers, like that."

"So?"

"So he said he didn't need anything but the AK-47s. I told him you can't have too much firepower, he said come down here, see Matt, take a look for myself. I'm impressed. But I still say you can't have too much."

The guard stayed wary. He said, "Why didn't he call ahead?" and patted the walkie-talkie attached to his belt.

"How should I know? He was busy, maybe that's why. Listen, you don't want me here, that's fine by me. I've seen enough." I started away from the box of grenades.

"You just hold it," he said.

I stopped again. "Why? What the hell?"

He kept looking at me, thinking over what I'd told him; the .45's muzzle was still on my belly. I stood there meeting his gaze, trying not to think about what a round from an automatic that size could do to a man's insides. Trying not to sweat.

Pretty soon I said, "Well? We gonna stand around here like this all frigging afternoon?"

"Go on in the office."

"Yeah, sure. What for?"

He motioned with his free hand. "Go on."

I put on a disgusted look; I thought it might work on him better than backtalk or a display of anger. A shrug, a headshake, and I walked into the office. He followed at a distance, stood in the inner doorway as I turned to face him again.

"Now what?"

"Now you sit down there. One of those chairs."

"Oh, for Chrissake. What's the big idea? I told you—"

"I know what you told me. I want to check with the Colonel."

"Where you think I got this badge?" I said. Heavy on the disgust this time. "Who the hell you think I am anyway?"

"I don't think anything," he said. "I just want to check with the Colonel. You got a problem with that?"

What could I say? "No problem. Just make it quick—I got better things to do with my time."

"Sit down there."

I moved sideways to the nearest folding chair, laid a hand on its back. But I didn't sit down. "I don't feel like parking my ass," I said. "*You* got a problem with that?"

Ten-second staredown. He ended it by reaching down with his free hand and unhooking the walkie-talkie from his belt.

Two choices again, both of them bad. I could try to catch him by surprise, disarm him, put him out of commission, then make a run for it down the escape road; or I could remain his prisoner, let him take me to the Colonel, and try to talk my way out of here. Damn poor odds, either way. Matt had nearly thirty years on me and he was in better physical shape; and I knew all too well the damage a .45 slug could inflict at close range. And I no longer had the verbal leverage I'd consoled myself with on the drive in: I'd seen the weapons stash, knew how extensive and illegal it was. They couldn't afford to let me walk out of there with that kind of knowledge, no matter how many people knew of my intention to breach the compound.

"Unit Nine to Unit One," Matt was saying into his walkie-talkie. "Unit Nine to Unit One. Do you copy, Unit One?"

I closed my fingers loosely around the back of the chair. If I could lift and pitch it at him with enough quickness . . .

Crackly static came out of the walkie-talkie. That was all—no answering voice.

Matt frowned and repeated his message.

Static. And more static.

His eyes bored into me as if he thought it was my fault the

Colonel wasn't responding. I pulled a face, mixing annoyance with the disgust, and shifted my feet a little—all in an effort to appear relaxed and unconcerned. Inside I was sparking heat and tension, like a box filled with overloaded high-voltage wires.

"Unit One, come in, Unit One . . ."

Crackle.

"So he's separated from his unit," I said. And I couldn't have asked for a better break. "You gonna keep me hanging here till you track him down?"

"Shut up."

"Don't tell me to shut up. It's your ass on the line here, pal, not mine. I'm telling you, the Colonel ain't gonna like you treating me this way. Neither will my people."

One, two, three beats. "Your people," he said. "Who are they?"

"Who do you think?"

"I'm asking you."

"Name Chaffee mean anything to you? How about the Colonel's brother-in-law?"

He blinked at me. They meant something, all right.

"Yeah, that's right," I said. "I drove up here from Modesto. Why don't you get somebody to contact Chaffee, too, while you're at it? Ask *him* if he knows Bill Anderson."

For the first time I could see little cracks in his soldier's stoicism. Wearing him down, I thought—but not enough, not yet.

"Unit Nine to Unit One, do you copy?"

Snap, crackle, and pop.

"Tell you what," I said. "How about if we just go find the Colonel ourselves, you and me? He's still somewhere in camp, it won't take us more than a few minutes—"

"I can't leave my post."

"Come on, man—"

"No," he said. "I can't leave my post."

The cracks were still there. The problem was, I'd used up all my bluff; there was nothing left I could say to finish the job. If I didn't act now, gamble with the cards I had, I might not have another chance.

Hard and angry, I said, "You can't leave your post, and the Colonel don't answer, and I'm supposed to just stand around here with a dumbass like you and a gun shoved in my face. Well, screw that. Enough's enough."

I took a step toward the door.

"Hold it. What do you think you're—"

"I'm leaving. No more crap."

"You're not going anywhere—"

"Yeah I am. You want to shoot me in the back, go ahead." Another step, turning away from him. "But you'll be dead meat too when the Colonel finds out. Guaranteed."

I kept on going, chills on my neck and back, the flesh crawling. *Never hear the shot that kills you.* I put my hand on the doorknob, turned it. Behind me I could hear Matt moving, his boots shuffling on the floor—but he didn't say anything more, didn't come after me as I opened the door, went through it into the gusting wind and rain. I resisted an impulse to throw it shut, left it wide open and kept on walking, head down, fighting another impulse to look back.

The walk through the mud and grass, across to where I'd left my car, seemed to take an impossibly long time—one of those dreamlike sequences in which every movement, every clock tick and heartbeat, happens at inchmeal speed. The road would not get any closer . . . but finally I was on the road. The car would not get any closer . . . but finally I was in the car, with the door shut and locked. The speed of things increased then, but not quite all the way; there still seemed to be a jerky, sluggish quality to my actions and perceptions.

Sweat and rain in my face, dripping; I wiped it away, looking out through the side window as I started the engine. Matt was over there in the doorway, watching me, the .45 in one hand and the walkie-talkie still clenched in the other. But now he was holding the weapon down at his side. I put the transmission in gear and pulled away, making a conscious effort to keep the pressure of my foot light on the accelerator. I stayed on the main road, bypassing the escape road, because if I'd gone that way, it would have tipped him sure.

It seemed to take another small eternity to reach the fork in front of the parade ground. I kept looking left and right, glancing up into the rearview mirror, expecting Jeeps and trucks, men with guns, to come rushing out in pursuit. Nothing happened. I turned onto the asphalt that led out to the main gate. Another glance in the mirror, and the entire camp was visible behind me—evil in the rain, eaten into the wilderness like a cancer—and then I was into the trees and it was gone. But its afterimage remained sharp and clear against the backs of my eyes.

One more gauntlet to run. Except that it turned out to be an anticlimax. The young blond sentry opened up right away when he saw me, both gates, and stood stiffly and touched his backward-turned cap in a kind of weak salute as I passed. The sorry bastard was still worried that I might have reported him for deserting his post.

My body wouldn't relax until I was a few miles along Timberline Road. And when the tension release came, it left me feeling enervated. Close back there—as close as I'd come to dying helpless in a long time. Foolish risk. Reckless, stupid, self-destructive . . .

Cut it out.

You went in there because it was something that needed doing. Part of the job, part of who you are. And you survived and that's the bottom line. Let it go at that.

Five seconds after I walked into number eleven at the Northern Comfort, the telephone bell went off. I let it ring three more times before I picked up.

Ruth Bartholomew's gin-rich voice said, "There's a message for you."

"Is that right? Must be pretty important."

". . . How's that?"

"For you to be watching out the window for me."

She made a sniffling sound. "Wasn't watching out for you," she said. "Just happened to see you drive in. You want your message or not?"

"Go ahead."

"Luke Judson called up. Wants you to call him."

"I don't know any Luke Judson."

"Owns Judson's Oasis, few miles up the highway."

"Did he say what he wanted?"

"No. I didn't ask neither. None of my—"

"I know. None of your business."

"That's right."

"What time did he call?"

"Around noon. Give you his number."

She did that and I wrote it down.

"He's a busybody," she said then.

"Luke Judson?"

"*He* don't mind his own business," she said. "You and him ought to get along real good."

I had a reply for that, but the line was already dead.

When I tapped out the number she'd supplied, a man's scratchy voice answered on the first ring. Instantly, as if he'd been sitting hunched over the phone. "Yeah, what is it?" Good old country cordiality. In the background I could hear a woman's shrill voice yelling and the back-sassing response of an equally shrill child.

"Luke Judson?"

"Who wants him?"

I told him who.

"Oh, yeah. Just a second." Away from the receiver he yelled, "Shut up, goddammit! Can't you see I'm on the phone?" The stridulous background exchange came to an abrupt end. And he said to me again, "About time you called up. I been waiting."

"What can I do for you, Mr. Judson?"

"Know something you want to know. Been thinking on it and I can't keep it to myself. Ain't right."

"What're we talking about?"

"Don't want to say it over the phone, with the wife and kid here. How about you come out in about an hour? Judson's Oasis, four miles north of town on Three ninety-five."

"How about you come here instead?"

"Can't do that," he said. "I got a bum leg and I ain't supposed to drive or move around too much. Hour okay?"

"No," I said.

". . . You say no?"

"I've got things to do that can't wait."

"Listen, what I got to tell you, it's real important. About them college kids you're looking for, the girl and the other one."

I glanced at my watch; the time was a couple of minutes past two-thirty. "Suppose we make it five o'clock."

"Five? Can't you get here sooner than that?"

"Best I can do, Mr. Judson."

There was a pause before he said, "All right, five. Oasis is closed until next month, but I live around back. Just drive on around and come in the house."

We rang off and I sat for a time, massaging my neck and stiff shoulder. The sense of enervation was gone, but the cold and the tension had me feeling my age. On the way there I'd thought hard about getting out of it right then—calling the FBI and Fassbinder, passing on what I'd found out and letting them take over; letting them dig out the connection between the Sentinels and Allison and Rob. But I couldn't quite make up my mind to do it that way. The need in me was too strong to finish what I'd started. For Helen McDowell's sake. And for my own.

In the bathroom I washed my hands and face, dried off, and took four aspirin for my various hurts. Then I zipped up the toilet kit, packed it in my suitcase; packed the rest of my stuff too, leaving nothing behind.

I'd parked the car in close to the cabin door, and when I

went out with the suitcase down low against my leg, the car's bulk shielded it from the office building and the street. I opened the passenger door, slid the case in on the seat. And then locked the cabin door before I got into the car.

I didn't stop at the office to check out or turn in the key. Maybe I wouldn't be back—and maybe I would. Either way, the less sure anybody in Creekside was of my whereabouts and intentions, the better off I would be.

18

Judson's Oasis was a high-roofed log building with a covered porch on two sides, set back fifty yards or so on the east side of the highway. A pole sign at the edge of a fronting asphalt lot next to the entrance drive gave the place's name in dead neon script; below that was a square with smaller, spaced words: FINE DINING DANCING LIVE MUSIC. I could tell that there was another building at a distance behind the main one, but it was dwarfed and I couldn't see enough of it through the dirty gray scrim of rain to estimate its size or shape. The property had a vacant look: no cars on the lot, no lights anywhere, not even a wisp of chimney smoke.

I slowed to forty-five as I passed, trying for a better far-side angle on the outbuilding. No dice: trees partially screened it to the north. Two or three vehicles could have been parked back there too; I wouldn't have been able to see them unless I drove in and around for a close look.

I stayed on the highway for another third of a mile, until I found a place where I could make a turn across the divider strip into the southbound lane. Traffic was sparse; mostly I had the rain-slick road to myself in both directions. When Judson's Oasis appeared again ahead, I began scanning the highway's near side. I thought I'd seen an intersection about fifty yards north of the Oasis, and I had: a country road that angled off to the west. I braked as soon as I spotted the sign for it, took the exit, and came off onto a narrow blacktop that climbed a rise between thinly spaced trees.

The side road was one piece of luck, and at the top of the rise was another—a flat, stony section that opened up to the south. The area was wide enough, and the hard earth and a carpeting of evergreen needles gave the surface enough traction in wet weather, for it to be used as both a turnaround and a parking spot; a crosshatching of recent tire tracks proved it. I turned in there, over close to the near end, where the trees grew down-slope to the highway verge. From that point I had a fairly good view through them and across to Judson's Oasis.

I left the engine running, got out long enough to open the trunk and snag my binoculars—a pair of powerful Zeiss 7 × 50. Inside again, I put the window down far enough so that I could rest the glasses on its edge. When I adjusted the focus I could see the Oasis all right, but I still couldn't make out much of the building behind it. So I backed the car a little ways, altered its angle slightly, and tried again. Better—much better. Now I had a mostly unobstructed view of about half the outbuilding: small, weathered A-frame with a side deck built on. The only visible window was curtained and shaded, a sightless eye. There was still no sign of life anywhere on the property, front or rear.

The rain kept coming down in a steady slant, which meant that I had to keep the window open partway in order to see clearly, which meant in turn that it grew damp and chilly in the car when I shut off the engine. But I couldn't leave it on to run the heater because I was low on gas. I buttoned my jacket to the throat, put on a pair of driving gloves to keep my fingers from numbing. Okay except for my ears; pretty soon they began to tingle. I got out again and poked around in the cluttered trunk until I found my old fisherman's hat. Ear problem solved.

I checked my watch. Five minutes past three.

With the binoculars on my lap, I settled down to wait.

It wasn't a long wait. Fifty-three minutes, give or take a few seconds.

I was in one of those states you drift into on stakeouts—body-shifting constantly to ease discomforts, alert but with your mental processes stuttery and sluggish—when the old primer-patched truck came barreling up the highway's northbound lane. As soon as I spotted it, even before it slowed to make the turn past the Judson's Oasis sign, I had the binoculars propped on the window edge and my eyes tight to the lenses.

The truck crossed the parking area, heading diagonally toward the main building's far corner. Despite a little rain-blur, the magnification brought it up close. Two men inside, Ollie Ballard at the wheel. The other man was less distinct through the rear window, but from the size and mostly hairless shape of his skull, I thought he must be Frank Hicks. And in the open rear bed—

Dogs. A brace of them, chained and muzzled.

Ballard's pit bulls.

The anger flared inside me, hot and raw. The bastards—the dirty bastards! Set a pair of blood-hungry fighting dogs on another human being, stand around watching while they ripped him apart. Just stand there and watch, for God's sake. No better than animals themselves. Worse, because they had nominal powers of reason.

Was that the way it happened with Allison and Rob?

The pit bulls snarling and tearing flesh while Ballard and Hicks stood there and watched?

The truck bucked along the north side of the Oasis, on past the A-frame and around behind it out of my sight. I worked the knobs on the glasses, trying for an even sharper focus. A minute passed. Two. Three. By the time the two men appeared on foot from behind the cabin, I had a tight check on the anger. Control was something I could not afford to relinquish now, not even for a little time.

The dogs, still muzzled and leashed, jumped and tugged and butted heads; Ballard was having a difficult time controlling them with both leashes wrapped around his right hand and wrist. His left wrist and forearm appeared tightly splinted and bandaged, the nonprofessional kind of doctoring. His scrawny face reflected the fact that he was in pain. I hope it hurts like fire, you son of a bitch, I thought. I hope it's just a taste of what's in store for your soul the day after you die.

The second man was Hicks, all right. He opened the A-frame's front door with a key, stood aside while Ballard herded the dogs inside, then followed and yanked the door shut after him. The key made me think of the fine upstanding family man I'd talked to on the phone . . . Luke Judson after all, or somebody who knew him well enough to borrow his house key. Yeah, and to get his permission to use the place as a slaughterhouse. Another Sentinel. Another candidate for the Pit.

I watched the A-frame for another five minutes. Neither Ballard nor Hicks reappeared. With them and the dogs shut away inside and the truck parked out of sight, Judson's Oasis once again wore its vacant look.

I'd been waiting for them: a sentinel for Sentinels. And now they were sitting in their trap waiting for me: Sentinels for the sentinel. Watchdogs, guardians of different sides of a societal coin, one representing the forces of order and justice, the other the forces of chaos and oppression. The irony was as bitter as camphor. But what made it easy to swallow was the knowledge that arrogance and stupidity would be their downfall, just as those things were the downfall of tyrants and knaves of every stripe. Sooner or later they all came crashing down into the rubble of their own arrogance and stupidity.

I put the binoculars in their case, started the car, and drove back down to the highway.

A wind was kicking up, strong and gusty enough out at the end of Spring Valley Road to buffet the car, turn the trees into a swaying chorus line. Ballard's squalid homeplace seemed even more flimsy under the wind's lash; when I negotiated the muddy access lane and left the car, I could hear boards and shingles rattling, creaking, moaning. A good big blow someday, I thought, and the whole damn shack would collapse.

Before I went up onto the porch I paused to satisfy myself that Ballard didn't have any more dogs lurking on the premises. If he did, they were mutes and passive besides: everything was quiet inside and in the dog run at the rear. I climbed the steps and tried the door. No reason for it to be locked way out here, and it wasn't. Ballard had nothing to fear from neighbors or strangers. Hell, it was the other way around.

I expected to find a junk-shop mess inside, but it wasn't quite that bad. Mismatched garage-sale furnishings, a few unclean dishes, kindling spilled out of a wood box, a scatter of newspapers that looked unread (he probably used them to light fires in the old wood-burning stove) and a filthy dog bed with splinters of bone and bits of gristled meat clinging to the fabric. The place smelled of dog. And of wood smoke, dampness, dry rot, old grease-laden meals.

One bare-wood wall was adorned with nude centerfolds probably torn out of *Playboy* and *Penthouse* and their raunchier cousins—all very white-skinned blondes and redheads with oversized breasts. Another wall was a sick paean to Ballard's racism. White flag with the Aryan Nations symbol and the words "Jew Busters" underneath. Poster: Four crossed and rope-bound axes surrounded by *Supreme* above, *White* on the left, and *Power* on the right. Poster: *USA Skinheads,* and a swastika, and a knife-bearing male Caucasian giving the Nazi salute, and the slogan "Let's Kick Some Ass!"

Yeah, I thought. Let's do that, Ollie, let's kick some ass. Yours and Hicks's and Darnell's and Slingerland's, for starters.

I prowled through the front room, the kitchen, a narrow screened-in sleeping porch. In each I had to resist an angry impulse to trash what I saw—the symbols of hate, specifically. Mindless destruction was their game; I wouldn't let myself play it. I opened drawers and cabinets, looked for hidey-holes, even got down and peered under the bed. It didn't take long, as small as the shack was.

I found two items of interest, both stuffed into a drawer in the kitchen. One was a blue and white felt triangle—Ballard's very own Sentinels badge. The other was a three-page computer-generated list of names and addresses, both of individuals and business establishments, in Modoc and Lassen counties. About a third of the names were Jewish; another third were Asian; the rest could have been of any nationality but were almost certainly those of African Americans and businesses owned by African Americans. The Sentinels' hit list. A few of the names had been roughly crossed out in ballpoint pen: targets already struck. One of those was a Vietnamese restaurant in Alturas, no doubt the same one DeFalco had told me about. I left the badge and the list in the drawer, reluctantly. By themselves they didn't prove a thing.

What I didn't find was what I'd gone there for: a single piece of evidence connecting Ballard to either Allison McDowell or Rob Brompton.

It frustrated me, because I'd read him as the type to keep souvenirs. There were examples scattered here and there to confirm that reading too: a twenty-year-old Oakland Raiders–Kansas City Chiefs game program, an array of shot glasses bearing the names of different bars and restaurants, a flyer from a KKK rally in southern Oregon, a business card from a member of the "Citizens' Law Enforcement & Research Committee" of the Portland branch of the Posse Comitatus, even a pair of torn woman's panties too old and too large to have belonged to Allison. If Ballard and Hicks had harmed Allison and Rob, with or without the damn pit bulls, he'd surely have kept some grisly little memento, wouldn't he?

On his own hook, he would. Hicks might be smart enough to have prevented it.

And what about Hicks? Would *he* have kept a memento?

I glanced at my watch. Not quite five yet. I had plenty of time before the pair of them realized I was not going to show up at the Oasis—at least an hour, possibly as much as two before they gave up on their trap. Enough time to scrounge Hicks's address, see if I could turn up anything incriminating at his home.

Except that he might not live alone, might have a family. Except that he hadn't struck me as the pack-rat type. Except that I wasn't up for any more frustration.

Except that I was no longer convinced Hicks and Ballard were guilty.

Of crimes real and planned against me, yes. Hard-line racists capable of murder with guns or pit bulls or any other lethal instrument—no question. No question, either, that they had to be aware of whatever had been done to Allison and Rob. But they did not have to be the perpetrators. There was another hand in this business, possibly more than one; if blood had been spilled, it might just be that those other hands were the stained ones.

I had an idea whose they were too.

The problem was the same as with Ballard and Hicks: proving it.

19

There was no way I would spend this night, or any more nights, in Creekside. I drove back through it in a hurry, out to the highway, and then straight down to Susanville to a Best Western I'd noticed on the outskirts. In my room, with the door locked, I took a quick shower, used the complimentary coffeemaker and two packets of french roast to brew a strong potful. When it was ready, I poured a cup and called Kerry at the condo. I needed to hear her voice—needed it bad. So it was relief as much as pleasure I felt when she picked up.

"You sound depressed," she said. "Things not going well up there?"

"Depends on your point of view. I made plenty of progress today, but it isn't the good kind." Not where Allison and Rob were concerned.

"Do you want to talk about it?"

"No. Not until it's finished."

"You're all right, though? I mean—"

"I know what you mean. Don't worry."

"How much longer will it take?"

"Hard to tell. Not too long."

"That's good, because I miss you."

"Me too you. Big-time."

"Shameless misses you too. He keeps running around looking for you. And giving me accusing looks, as if he thinks I might've done something to you."

"Nothing you could do to me that he wouldn't like."

"Well, maybe one or two things."

We talked for a while, neutral topics that mattered only to us. It wasn't until after we'd rung off that I realized I had neglected to tell her about Eberhardt's call. More evidence that I was not ready at any level to deal with him again. I wondered briefly if I ever would be, if I would bother to return his call before Sunday, or at all.

I drank coffee, feeling blue and lonely again, the anger simmering underneath like hot sulphur and brimstone. Should I call Helen McDowell? I couldn't bring myself to do it. She would be hurt and anxious if she didn't hear from me . . . I still couldn't do it. I was afraid something in my voice would give away the bleak suspicions that had piled up, their almost certain validity. Robbing her of the last of her hope before I was positive was a far greater cruelty than silence.

I did call DeFalco. He'd get antsy if I didn't, decide something had happened to me, and likely take matters into his own hands. As it was, once I finished filling him in on the day's events, he began lobbying for an immediate call to the FBI's San Francisco district office.

"Not just yet, Joe. I need a little more time."

"You can't sit on it," he said, "not now. It's too hot. If that weapons-stash guard told Darnell about you, he knows the camp's been breached."

I admitted that I may have botched things as far as the Colonel was concerned. But then I said, "If he was told and the fugitive warrant is his top priority, he's already long gone. I don't think that's the case, though. He's a tough mercenary soldier as well as a racist; I can't see him cutting and running and leaving all that artillery behind. Which he'd have to do. There's too much to move out in a hurry, and too much distance from the Corner to anyplace that would be safe."

"You've got a point," DeFalco agreed. "Darnell's more likely to fort up and make a fight of it. Another Waco or Ruby Ridge."

"Christ, I hope not with the same outcome or repercussions."

"Doubtful. The feds are under too much pressure and too media shy these days to get their asses in that kind of wringer again. Still, the situation could get nasty. Either way, it's hot news."

"It'll be just as hot if it goes down tomorrow."

"That all the extra time you want? One day?"

"Less. Say until noon. I'm close to the truth about the kids—real close. I can feel it."

"You sure it wasn't the Sentinels who were responsible?"

"Reasonably sure it wasn't Darnell or anybody at the camp. I've got a pretty good idea who. What I need is the right scenario and some hard evidence."

"And you figure you can get it by noon tomorrow?"

"If I can't, I'll let the feds take over."

"Okay," he said. "But if I don't hear from you by noon, I'll phone the FBI myself. That's a promise."

I sat around for a time, drinking coffee and trying to assemble the bits and pieces of information I'd gathered into a cohesive whole. It was the chain of circumstances—where the crimes had happened, how, what had triggered them—that kept hanging me up. I was pretty sure I had enough pieces, but the key ones eluded me.

At eight o'clock I gave it up and went out to the coffee shop adjacent to the motel, where I ate a tasteless coffee shop meal and lingered over two more cups of bitter brew. Back in the room I tried watching something on TV to give my mind a rest. But there was nothing in any of the flickering images and inane dialogue to hold my attention for more than a few seconds, much less to distract me. I shut the thing off and drew a hot bath and soaked in the tub for the better part of an hour. It didn't help my thought processes, but it did relax me enough to make me drowsy.

I crawled into bed—and I was wide awake again. I lay there watching the dark. Finally, somewhere around midnight, the jumble in my head settled enough so I could sleep.

And dream. And dream . . .

Churches. Old white one in Creekside, dark unpainted one in the Sentinels' camp. Crosses outlined against gray sky. Crosses burning. Someone screaming. Black man wearing a crown of thorns, arms and legs torn and bleeding, spread-eagled on a cross . . .

I woke up suddenly in a cold sweat. Four A.M. by the bedside clock radio. And my subconscious had worked to make it all clear in my conscious mind, the whole sequence of events as they must have taken place two weeks ago. Who, what, where, when, why . . . everything.

And the worst of it was, the whole truth had been in my head, and under and over my head, for long days and longer nights. Monsters hiding in plain sight that I simply had not recognized for what they were.

Christ.

And thinking that was bad too, because He shouldn't have been a part of it and He was.

Creekside at five-thirty on a Sunday morning was a ghost town—a place where there were whispers and twitches of life, but a dying place just the same. The deserted main drag was layered with wind gathers of leaves and evergreen needles and Saturday-night litter. The closed-up buildings had a gone-and-forgotten aspect, like the ones on the two defunct farms far out on Spring Valley Road. Even the scatter of night lights seemed spectral, paled and fuzzed by the ceaseless rain and the pre-dawn cloud cover.

I rolled along slow with my headlights off, not trying to avoid any of the water-filled potholes. When I jounced past Trilby's Hardware & Supply, the only light ahead was the one illuminating the Northern Comfort sign a block and a half distant. At the corner I turned into the side street that dead-ended to the east—the one I'd crossed on foot Tuesday evening, just before Colonel Benjamin Darnell's Jeep driver had nearly run me down.

Most of the block-long street was flanked with trees, those on the north running in an unbroken line and creating a thick screen that cut off any view of the motel cabins, even blotted out the light on the sign. One house, bungalow size, squatted on the south side near the corner; no lights showed in any of its windows. Another stand of pine and Douglas fir separated the house from the block's second building, a sagging barn or large shed at the far end. Fifteen or twenty yards past the building, a rusted metal guard rail marked the street's terminus.

I pulled up next to the building—a barn decrepit enough to have once been a livery, the remnants of a Bull Durham sign painted on its near wall. I got out into the cold drizzle, leaving the engine running; hugged the shadows to the barn's far corner and poked my head around it. Between the side wall and the end of the street was a section of tall grass and nothing else. No Bronco, no primer-patched truck, no vehicle of any kind. But one had been parked there not too long before: in close to the barn some of the grass was mashed down in a pair of ten-foot-long parallel strips. This was where Hicks and Ballard had hidden their wheels before Friday night's ambush.

I followed one of the tire tracks a short way, to test the ground. A little soft and muddy after the continual rainfall, but still firm enough so you didn't need to worry about a car getting mired. I looked out beyond the guard rail. The creek flowed there, fast and noisy between low banks. It was maybe ten yards wide at this point.

When I had the car pulled in alongside the barn, following the tracks in the grass, I unhooked the six-cell flashlight and slipped it into my left coat pocket. It made a clinking sound against the two screwdrivers I'd taken from the toolbox in the trunk before leaving Susanville. The weight of the .38 was a cold comfort in the other pocket.

I slogged through the wet grass to the creek. When I glanced back I could barely see the car parked in the shadows. Fitting, by God. And nobody would know I was back in this miserable little hamlet until I wanted them to know it.

I turned north along the near creekbank, followed its meandering progress into the woods. The earth grew spongy, almost boggy in spots; I walked slow to maintain my footing, in a hunch with eyes downcast, but I couldn't see much except shapes and outlines. Even though it was nearing dawn and the sky was beginning to lighten a little, the tall pines cradled the darkness as if reluctant to let go of the night. Twice, when I encountered tree-root snarls and juts of rock, I had to drag out the flash and switch it on briefly, shielded by my hand, to find my way around the obstacles.

It took me more than twenty minutes to work my way to where the trees thinned and I could make out the rearmost of the motel cabins. I veered away from the creek at that point, on a long diagonal to the back wall of cabin eleven, moving as swiftly as the footing permitted. Making noise was not a problem; the trees dripped rainwater in a steady cadence that was surprisingly loud in the early morning stillness.

From the back wall I eased around to the bathroom window on the south side, laid my ear against cold glass. If there were any sounds inside, the dripping trees shut them out too. At the front corner I paused again, this time to reconnoiter. The grounds had the same dead-and-gone aspect as the rest of Creekside. The one visible window in the Bartholomews' living quarters was lightless, and I neither saw nor smelled wood smoke. Not even those two seemed to be up and around this early.

I moved over next to the front window. The shade was up about six inches at the bottom—the way I'd left it?—but when I bent and squinted I couldn't see anything within except a thick gloom. An ear to the glass didn't pick up anything either. Chances were nobody was waiting for me in there, or I would have found Hicks's Bronco or Ballard's truck parked next to the barn; but I'd had enough surprises and taken enough risks. I drew the .38, held the cabin key in my left hand, worked the key quietly into the lock, and went in fast and low with the gun at arm's length.

Empty.

I shut and locked the door, lowered the shade all the way to ensure complete privacy. A quick look around the room and the bathroom cubicle told me nothing, but I'd have given odds that somebody had been in there since my departure yesterday—checking after I failed to show up at Judson's Oasis. The absence of my luggage, even though I hadn't checked out and turned in my key, must have confused them, kept them from setting up another ambush. They couldn't be sure I intended to come back.

The room was packed with chill. And the cold rain and the long trek through the woods had left me wet, my fingers and toes numbed. I turned on the space heater to its highest setting, shucked out of coat and shoes and socks, used one of the threadbare bathroom towels to dry off. I laid the shoes and socks in front of the heater; sat on the floor with them until my blood began circulating freely again.

The gun went into my belt, the first I'd let it out of one hand or the other since I'd entered. I took the flashlight and screwdrivers from my coat, did what needed to be done with them, and found what I expected to find. Then I pulled the chair over between the heater and the window, crimped an edge of the shade just enough to create an eyehole, and sat down to another wait.

20

The vigil, this time, lasted a little better than two hours.

Church bells commenced pealing, faint above the up-and-down babble of the wind, about eight-thirty. The Bartholomews had been up for an hour and a half by then; at least, seven was when the light had gone on in what I took to be their kitchen. The bells had been making their musical summons for nearly five minutes when the two of them came out through the rear door.

He was dressed in a shiny dark blue suit that fit him like a sack, his tie drawn so tightly his wattles hung down in folds alongside the knot; she wore a black and white dress and a boxy hat with some kind of feather poking out of it. On their way to Sunday services. Both together, because as far as they knew they didn't have any guests, so there was no reason they shouldn't close the motel office for an hour or so.

One hand tight on his wife's arm, Ed Bartholomew helped her into their old Buick. She was a little unsteady on her feet—the muddy ground over there, or more likely a few belts of pre-sermon gin. I watched him fold himself stiffly behind the wheel, start the engine, let it warm up for a minute or so, then maneuver the car around the building and out onto Main Street. He was a good driver, not too fast, not too slow, with a sure touch on the wheel.

I waited five more minutes, in case they'd forgotten something. When they didn't come back I worked some of the stakeout kinks from my shoulders and back, put on socks and shoes—mostly dry now—and my coat, and went out into the cold morning. The rain had quit again for the time being, but still more was on the way: the smell and feel of wet clogged the air, and dark clouds swarmed overhead. I picked my way across the courtyard, around puddles that had grown and flowed together to form miniature lakes. The street out front was deserted now.

Bartholomew had locked the rear door, but it was not much of a lock; even with my sore finger I had it picked in less than thirty seconds. Another five and I was inside.

Kitchen, as I'd thought. Breakfast aromas lay heavy in the too-warm room—toast, sausages, fried eggs, coffee. Strong in there, too, was the juniper berry smell. Next to the sink, an empty orange juice carton and an empty Gordon's bottle bore silent witness.

There were three other rooms: living room, bedroom, bathroom. All were cramped and in need of tidying and a thorough dusting and sweeping. The bedroom was where I started, for no reason except a feeling that it was the right choice. And it was.

On the nightstand between twin beds lay a well-used Gideon Bible; and on the wall above an oak dresser hung both a brass crucifix and a painting of a thorn-crowned Christ not unlike the one above the bed in cabin eleven. Symbols of faith, symbols of love. Directly underneath, in two of the dresser drawers, I found the symbols of hate.

They were different in type from the ones in Ollie Ballard's shack, but not different in kind. Computer-generated leaflets and pamphlets—desktop publishing of the worst kind. Recent issues of newspapers: *The California Klan News,* the Posse Comitatus's *Posse Noose Report,* the White Aryan Resistance's *Aryan Vigil,* the Christian National Emancipation League's *Sentinels of Light.* Cheaply printed paperback books, two with swastikas and death heads on their covers: *Warrant for Genocide, Hitler Was Right!, White Power—Dead Coons,* and the inspiration and blueprint for the Oklahoma City bombing atrocity, *The Turner Diaries*. Clipped articles and bumper-sticker-style slogans: "White People Built This Country—White People Are This Country." "Niggers and Kikes Beware!" "Make a List of Your Enemies." "Arm Yourselves Before It's Too Late." "The Only Way to Be Free of What Threatens You Is to Kill It—Learn to Kill Now!"

Jesus above and death below. It made me feel cold again, and unclean, and sad and angry and a little awed. How do they reconcile it? I thought. Pictures of the Savior, crucifix, Bible on the nightstand, and garbage like this tucked away in drawers. Read a little from the Book of Genesis or the Book of Job, then read a little from *White Power—Dead Coons*. How in God's name do they reconcile religion and sacrilege, brotherhood and genocide?

Maybe they don't, I thought then. Maybe the only way they can live with their contrary beliefs is to not even try. And maybe that's why she swills gin, why he has the look of a reanimated corpse, why they live like this, why they did the things they did. Caught between two polar opposites, push-pull, for months and years until they were incapable of making any rational distinction; until they were self-indoctrinated to the point of paranoid schizophrenia. Now all they could do was respond to one set of stimuli or the other—love or hate, life or death, the Christian way or the racist way, but never one in relation to the other.

I was sweating now and my stomach had begun to churn up bile. I wanted out of this place, into the cold, clean air outside. But not until I had the rest of what I'd come for.

The bedroom held nothing more for me. Neither did the living room. In a closet off the kitchen I found a pump shotgun, a Winchester .30-30, and a pre–World War II Savage with iron sights. All three weapons were loaded, and in there with them were at least a hundred additional rounds of ammunition for each—as if the Bartholomews were expecting a siege. "Arm

Yourselves Before It's Too Late." "The Only Way to Be Free of What Threatens You Is to Kill It—Learn to Kill Now!" Yeah. A siege was exactly what they were expecting.

I hunted for a handgun. No handgun. But there had to be at least one somewhere on the premises . . . the right one. They would not have gotten rid of it, not people like them, not under any circumstances. Waste not, want not, when you're learning how to kill.

I located it out front, in a drawer under the office counter—a .32 Iver Johnson revolver, clean and oiled and fully loaded. The evidence I'd found in cabin eleven said that the murder gun had to be a .32 or a small-bore .38. Not much doubt that this was it.

Without touching the revolver, I shut the drawer and continued my search. The pocket of a fleece-lined jacket hanging from a hook on the kitchen wall yielded one more piece of hard evidence—two pieces, actually. Greyhound bus ticket stubs, both stamped with dates thirteen days earlier, one from Eureka to Redding and the other from Redding to Susanville.

When I finished examining the stubs, I returned them to the jacket pocket. If Bartholomew hadn't gotten rid of them in the past two weeks, he wouldn't think to do it when he got home from church; it was likely he'd forgotten he still had them. The stubs would be much more damning if the authorities found them just as I had.

Done.

I opened the back door, didn't see anybody in the courtyard, reset the lock, and stepped outside. But I was wrong about the area being deserted—wrong twice, going in and now coming out. I hadn't advanced more than a few paces when a familiar voice said, "You hold it right there," and froze me in midstride.

Art Maxe.

Standing ten feet away, at the corner by the covered woodpile, with a deer rifle pointed at my head.

I was damned tired of being confronted by people brandishing guns. But there wasn't much I could do about it in this case other than what I'd done on the previous instances—try to talk myself out of harm's way. The .38 might still have been in the car for all the chance I had of defending myself with it. I kept my hands down at my sides—I couldn't have gotten the left one up very high anyhow as sore as my shoulder was—and stood waiting to see what Maxe would do.

He took a couple of strides in my direction. "What the hell you been up to in there?"

"What do you think I've been up to?"

"I saw you break in from down the road. Good thing I keep this rifle in my truck. What'd you steal?"

"Nothing."

"The hell. You took something, got it on you. County cops'll find it, by God."

So it wasn't in his head to shoot me. Maybe I was wrong about him, the extent of his involvement—maybe. "Go ahead and call Captain Fassbinder," I said. "I was just about to do it myself."

"Sure you were."

"Plain truth. I found what I was after."

"Yeah? What's that?"

"All the evidence Fassbinder will need."

"Evidence? What evidence?"

"That the Bartholomews murdered Allison McDowell and Rob Brompton two weeks ago last night."

The rifle's muzzle dipped a few inches; he stared at me as if I'd suddenly changed shape, sprouted tentacles and eyestalks. "You're crazy as a barn owl," he said.

"We both know I'm not."

"Ed Bartholomew? Ruth? I've known them thirty years . . . they wouldn't kill nobody."

"One of them did. Or both together."

"Why? Chrissake, why would they?"

"Because Rob Brompton was black. Because they're the kind of racists who believe the only way to be free of what threatens them is to kill it."

Maxe shook his head, more in confusion than negation. "They're mixed up with the Sentinels? Ed and Ruth?"

"Sentinels, Christian National Emancipation League, Posse Comitatus—name the hate group, and they belong to it. But not you, huh, Maxe?"

"Me? You still think I'm into that shit?"

"Not if you keep denying it."

"Damn right I deny it. I told you, I don't belong to no organizations. Sure, I went to one of the meetings out at the Sentinels' camp, see what they were all about. But I didn't like what I heard. Still don't. I never went back."

"So you don't know about Frank Hicks and Ollie Ballard?"

"Know what about 'em? You saying they're Sentinels too?"

"Sentinels, and thick as thieves with the Bartholomews. The two of them jumped me Friday night, and when that didn't work, they tried again yesterday afternoon."

"You mean they tried to kill you?"

"Not the first time. Just put me out of commission. They were waiting in one of the other cabins when I got back here from Susanville—had to be inside a cabin because it was raining and their clothes smelled dry and felt dry. The Bartholomews set it up. How else would Hicks and Ballard get a key to an empty cabin?"

"Jesus Christ."

"The Bartholomews worked the setup yesterday, too, with a phony phone call. Those two pit bulls of Ballard's would have taken me out permanently if I hadn't seen through the trap."

Another headshake. Maxe was no mental giant; his faculties were overloaded, his confusion too plain to be anything but genuine.

"It happened, Maxe, everything I've told you. Believe it—the parts you don't already know about."

"What parts? Listen, I didn't have nothing to do with *anything* like that. I was home Friday and yesterday afternoon. Ask my wife, she'll tell you—"

"All right, so you weren't involved in the attempts against me. Or directly involved with the murders. But there's still the matter of Allison's MG. You had to be in on that, no mistake."

"Bullshit. What're you talkin' about now?"

"You lied to the law and to me about Allison and Rob picking up her car Sunday morning. They couldn't have picked it up—they were already dead by then. Why'd you lie if you had nothing to do with getting the MG out of Creekside and over to Eureka?"

"Eureka? What's this about Eureka?"

"Why'd you lie, Maxe?"

"Ed . . . he come down to the garage that morning. Asked if their car was ready, said if it was he'd take it back to the motel. Said the kids was still in bed and he wanted to get rid of 'em and if he brought their car right up to the door, that'd tell them they wasn't wanted."

"And you believed him?"

"Why shouldn't I? He never lied to me before."

"Why'd he say he wanted to be rid of them?"

"Him and Ruth didn't like the idea of a white girl and a black man sleeping together in one of their cabins. Said he wouldn't've put 'em up if he'd known the boy was a nigger. Said he didn't find it out until just that morning or he'd have sent 'em packing sooner. . . ." Maxe wet his lips. Then, explosively, "Shit!"

"So you let Bartholomew have the MG. What'd he say then?"

"Then?"

"To convince you to lie about who picked it up."

"Said he didn't want anybody to know he was fetching their car for them, didn't want anybody saying Ed Bartholomew fetched for a nigger and his white whore."

"Those were the words he used?"

"Exact words."

"And you didn't know he was a racist?"

"All right, maybe I did. But not about him and Ruth belonging to the Sentinels or those other groups. Anyhow, he put it to me as a favor—not telling about him fetching the MG. I didn't see no harm in it. Why should I? So I said all right, if anybody asked I'd say the kids come and got it themselves." Maxe wiped mist off his face with the back of his free hand. The rifle hung slackly in his other hand, its muzzle now aimed at the ground between us. "Ed drove the MG all the way to Eureka, is that it?"

"That same day sometime. Abandoned it there to make it look like that was where Allison and Rob disappeared. On Monday he took a bus from Eureka to Redding and another from Redding to Susanville; I found the ticket stubs inside. His wife must have picked him up in Susanville. She drives, doesn't she?"

"Yeah," Maxe said. "Not too far, way she drinks, but Susanville . . . yeah." His head waggled again loosely, like a bulb atop a broken plant stem. "I still can't hardly believe . . . What'd they do to them kids? I mean, how'd they—?"

"Shot them."

"Where?"

"Cabin eleven. Same one I've been staying in."

"How you know that? How you know they used a gun?"

"Come over there with me and I'll show you."

I started away, not hurrying. Maxe stayed put for a few seconds and then fell into step beside me, still carrying the rifle muzzle downward in one hand.

Inside the cabin I said, "Everything's old in here—bed frame, dresser, TV, pictures on the walls. Everything except the mattress. That's brand new."

"So what? Mattresses wear out."

"Wasn't the case here. Bartholomew replaced the old one because it had bloodstains and bullet holes."

"Just guessing," Maxe said. "Ain't you?"

"No. There's something else that proves it. That picture of Christ over the bed . . . why was it hung off center that way, down so low?" I went over and lifted the picture down. It had been screwed to the wall, but I'd removed the screws earlier. I pointed and said, "That's why."

He stared at the hole in the wall—the little round hole that had been hastily patched with wood putty but whose size and shape were still discernible. The little round hole that had been made by a .32-caliber bullet from the Bartholomews' Iver Johnson revolver. I stared at it too, as I had at four A.M. and with the same thought in my mind: I'd spent three nights in this room, on the same bed if on a different mattress. The thought started my skin crawling again; I shook it out of my mind.

"He dug the slug out before he patched it," I said. "But the hole itself is enough. Added to the other evidence, it's more than enough."

Maxe's face was creased like a hound's. "Just come over here in the night and blew them away?" he said with the same kind of awe I'd felt earlier in the Bartholomews' bedroom. "Just like that?"

"I don't know for sure about that part of it. It might have been premeditated, or maybe something happened to set off one or both of them. We'll find out later."

"And after it was done? What'd Ed do with the bodies?"

"Hauled them away somewhere. Buried them. We'll find that out later too."

There was the sound of a car in the courtyard, crunching through the wet gravel. Maxe turned into the open doorway. Past him I could see the old Buick splash over to the rear of the office building, come to a stop. When Ed Bartholomew got out and started around to the passenger side, Maxe set off in a fast walk that quickened until he was almost running. I called, "Maxe, wait," but he didn't listen or stop. All I could do was to chase after him.

Both Bartholomews were out of the car, standing on the passenger side, him with his hand on his wife's arm, when Maxe reached them. They looked at him, at me coming up behind, at him again. There was nothing in Ed Bartholomew's eyes, no emotion of any kind. If he was a closed book, Ruth Bartholomew was a wide-open one with a cracked binding: still unsteady on her feet, cheeks so pale the rouge on them was like daubs of crimson paint, eyes ablaze when they rested on me. She'd left all her love at the church. Now that she was home again, with her need for gin clawing at her, she had redonned her hate like a grotesque mask.

Bartholomew said, "What you doing here with that rifle, Art? And with *him*?" as I came up. "What's going on?"

Maxe glanced at the rifle as if he'd forgotten he was carrying it. I thought he might blurt out the fact that I'd been prowling inside their home, but he didn't. Nodding at me he said, "He thinks you done something to the college kids. *Killed* them, for Chrissake, over in number eleven."

It came out slap-hard, but neither of the Bartholomews reacted to it. There was not even a flicker of change in Ed Bartholomew's stoic expression. His wife's eyes seemed to get hotter, brighter—that was all. Neither of them said anything. The silence among the four of us was cold and dead, like night hush in a graveyard.

"Well, Ed? You got anything to say?"

Bartholomew said, "No, I ain't," and turned and tried to prod his wife into walking away with him. She resisted. She had something to say.

"What's the matter with you, Art Maxe?" she demanded. Shrill-voiced, like a harpy. "You turning against your own kind? You're one of us, you're a God-fearing white man. He's an outsider and a nigger lover. What in the Lord's name is wrong with you?"

Maxe didn't answer. He looked a little sick.

Bartholomew pushed the woman this time, using his body, and got her swung around and moving toward the kitchen door. But she wasn't done talking yet. She called out over her shoulder, "Don't you listen to him. You're one of us, you *are*, and don't you ever forget it. We're the same, Art Maxe—we're birds of a feather!"

They were at the door by then. And a few seconds later they were out of my sight.

"We ain't the same," Maxe said to me. Then he said, "You were right. They done it."

21

I left Maxe to keep an eye on things and walked to the general store and made two calls on the public phone: the Lassen Sheriff's Department and Joe DeFalco. Fassbinder wasn't in but the officer I spoke to said he'd contact him; and DeFalco, sounding ecstatic, said he would take care of notifying the FBI and the Bureau of Alcohol, Tobacco, and Firearms. When I was finished with the calls I went and rounded up my car and drove it to the Northern Comfort and waited with Maxe for the law to show up.

The Bartholomews did not try to run. Nor did they arm or barricade themselves inside their home. They didn't do anything except maybe guzzle some gin, read the Bible, and curse me and my kind. I would have been surprised if they'd tried to run or to make a fight of it. It was one thing to take up weapons against what you believed was a coming race war, a kind of unholy war; it was an entirely different thing to flee from or take up weapons against White Authority. Particularly when in their warped way of thinking they really hadn't done anything wrong.

In a sense that was the most terrible fact of all: Ed and Ruth Bartholomew truly did not believe they had done anything wrong.

They made their confessions to Fassbinder and the county sheriff himself at twelve-fifteen that afternoon. I wasn't there when they opened up under questioning; Maxe and I were back at his garage, waiting there and mostly avoiding each other because there was nothing left to say. One of the deputies came and told us. But I did get to see the transcriptions of their statements later on, and each one made me glad I had not been present to see and hear the words spew out of their mouths.

Ruth Bartholomew: *They were making noise over in eleven, laughing and whooping, just having themselves a gay old time. Wasn't anybody else staying with us that night, so you could hear them plain. I went on over to see what they was up to. A body has to be careful in the motel business. Sometimes guests get rowdy, break things, steal things, you got to watch them like a hawk. The shade was up partway and the window was wide open, they didn't even have the decency to pull the shade or close the window all the way, and there they were inside for all the world and the devil to see, naked as the day they was born, laughing and rolling around on the bed, him with his big black member sticking straight up in the air. Well, I was never so shocked in all my life. Never seen nothing so lewd and disgusting. White girl and that big buck nigger . . . we never even knew she was with a nigger. Ed never seen him when they checked in and neither did I, not until I looked in that window and my eyes was seared by the sight of them, kissing and fondling one another on one of my beds, practically in my own Christian house. Well, it just made me go off my head. Make any decent white person lose his senses, an abomination like that. I don't remember going in for the pistol. Next thing I knew I had it in my hand and I was opening the cabin door, they never bothered to lock the door neither, and then I was right there in the room with 'em. I don't remember shooting her. Him, though . . . two rounds right in the middle of his dirty black face. Oh, I remember that, all right. I'll never forget that. Sorry? No, I ain't sorry. Why should I be sorry? What they was doing, him and his white whore, they was sinning against the whole white Christian race, against God Himself. They deserved what I gave them . . . I was God's own avenging angel, sent to smite them down. I'd do it again the same way if God give me the chance. I'd do it all again the same way!*

Ed Bartholomew: *They was already dead, both of them, when I run in. Wasn't much for me to do except clean up the mess and get Ruth calmed down. I wrapped 'em up in blankets and put 'em in the car. Mattress and sheets too, on account of all the blood. Hurt my back doing all that heavy lifting, my back's been paining me fierce ever since. Then I took 'em out in the woods and dug a hole and put them in it. No, not too far from here, just a few miles over east. Next morning I got their little sports car from Art Maxe and put their belongings in it and drove it over to Eureka and left it there and come back on the bus. I guess that's all. I ain't sorry it happened neither. Like Ruth said, what they were doing was a sin and an abomination and she was the instrument of God's judgment against it. I don't see nothing to be sorry for.*

Bartholomew took Fassbinder and the sheriff to where he'd buried the bodies in a shallow common grave. I wasn't there for that, either; there was no way I would have gone along even if I'd been invited. Nor would I go along when they went to arrest Frank Hicks and Ollie Ballard, though I damned well intended to press charges against both men for aggravated assault and, if it could be made to stick, intent to commit murder.

Before the law left with Bartholomew, I got permission to quit Creekside for the time being. Later on there would be quite a party and I would have to be there for it. DeFalco had said he would grab a photographer and hire a plane and be up in four or five hours. And FBI and ATF agents and federal marshals would soon be showing up in bunches. Whether or not they decided to raid the Sentinels camp was a moot point at this stage; they had to act slowly and carefully these days, after the public furor over their screwups with the Branch Davidian in Waco and the Ruby Ridge shootout in northern Idaho. Whatever they did about Darnell and the Sentinels, Chaffee and the Christian National Emancipation League, it didn't really involve me. I'd done my duty, and once I answered a battery of official questions, I would be out of it.

There was plenty of time before the big party started, and I had no stomach for making my last call of the day from this ugly little village with its ugly little people. I wanted no more to do with it or them from now on than was absolutely necessary—any of them, including Lena and Mike Cermak and Art Maxe. So I drove to the Best Western in Susanville and made my last call from there. The hard one, the one I'd been dreading all day. The one to tell Helen McDowell, as Fassbinder would have to tell Rob Brompton's parents, of the unconscionable evil that had destroyed a pair of innocent young lives.

22

The Sentinels, organized unit and camp both, came to a sudden termination early Monday morning. The FBI and ATF were partly responsible, but in the main the bastards simply self-destructed. And it all happened more or less bloodlessly, much to the evident relief of local law, local residents, and beleaguered feds.

DeFalco and I were both wrong about how the Sentinels' brain trust would react when they found out the compound had been breached and a government raid was imminent. In the first place, those intellectual giants, Colonel Darnell and Reverend Slingerland, didn't put it together until around noon on Sunday. And when they did figure it out, there was a sharp disagreement as to what to do about it. Darnell had wanted to fort up for a siege, all right, but his second-in-command was against it; Slingerland's solution was to load up as much of the arsenal as could be crammed into the three large trucks they had available and make a run for it. The dispute turned heated, tempers frayed and snapped, guns came out, triggers got yanked, and when the smoke cleared, the Colonel was dead and Slingerland had a flesh wound in his left arm.

The irony in this part was about as pretty as it gets. DeFalco even found grim humor in the shootout. A "black comedy in whiteface," he called it.

With Darnell dead, the camp was in a turmoil. Some of the Sentinels refused to leave, but most followed the good reverend's lead. The boxes of weapons and ammunitions were hauled out of the armory and loaded into the three trucks, which around two A.M. set out along the escape road on a run for Highway 395 south of Creekside. They never made it. The feds had the escape route pinpointed by then and they'd closed it off; they were waiting with plenty of men and firepower of their own. Slingerland was in the first truck and evidently unwilling to risk death again for his cause: he surrendered at the first show of force. The rest of the runaway pack quit, too, without much more than a couple of warning shots being fired.

A few hours later, just after another wet, gray dawn, the feds mobilized again and a hundred or so FBI and ATF agents and U.S. marshals, armed with federal warrants among other things, stormed the compound from both directions. They were met with token resistance. By that time only twenty people were left in the camp, and half of those were women and children; the rest had scattered into the woods. The remainder of the weapons stash was in government hands within an hour of the offensive.

When word of this came in to the Sheriff's Department in Susanville, where DeFalco and I were waiting, he turned to me and offered another of his cynical comments. It was apt, though. It summed the whole business up in a nutshell.

"With a whimper, not a bang," he said.

What with the vanquishing of the Sentinels and other matters, I didn't get around to calling Tamara Corbin until late that morning, after she'd come in to open up the office. And that was a foolish mistake on my part. She was hurt and angry, and she had every right to be—for more reasons than one.

"I sat around the whole weekend waiting on the phone to ring," she said. "Po' li'l black chile waitin' to hear from the massuh."

I said, "I should've called—you're absolutely right and I'm sorry. But there wasn't anything you could've done, and things got to be pretty crazy up here—"

"Yeah, I guess they did. I read Joe DeFalco's story in the paper this morning. All about it in the fucking *paper*. I ought to be grateful you called up this morning, huh?"

"Tamara . . ."

"Listen," she said, "it's shit, you know that? It's all shit and it's never gonna be anything else. You hear what I'm saying to you?"

"I hear."

"Whitey's world. Now and forever, amen."

"I don't believe that. I don't think you do either."

"No? You think the world doesn't belong to whitey? You really believe it's gonna be different someday?"

"Someday, yes."

"So you're satisfied with the way things turned out up there, right? All those big bad racist folks brought down. System works, justice triumphs again."

"Tamara," I said, "I'm one man. I did a one-man job the best way I knew how—that's all. No, I'm not satisfied. And you're wrong if you think it doesn't hurt me that Allison and Rob died the way they did, that I couldn't do anything to save them."

"They never had a chance anyway," she said bitterly. "Not once they took up with each other."

"You're wrong about that too. It wasn't just bigotry that killed them; it was circumstances. Circumstances kill people every day, no matter what color they are."

"Yeah, circumstances. They'd still be alive if they were both white."

"Or if their car hadn't quit on them when and where it did. Or if they hadn't been so much in love, they couldn't keep their hands off each other. Or if a dozen, a hundred, other things had happened differently."

"Okay, maybe. But I'm telling you, man, it'd still have been bad for them down the line. I know interracial couples. I know what kind of *circumstances* they can expect."

"If they'd loved each other enough—"

"What's this now, the love's-the-answer-to-everything rap? You and Dr. King. Only they killed him too, didn't they."

"So what's the alternative, Tamara? Be a hater like James Earl Ray? Like the Bartholomews and Colonel Darnell and Richard Chaffee and the rest of them? Hate sure as hell won't change the world."

She was quiet for several beats. "Love won't change it either," she said, but her anger seemed to have lost some of its intensity.

"It's already changing. Slow, too damn slow, but it is changing. It will change."

"Believe it when I see it."

"Just don't turn into a hater until you do. Let the bigots and the fools rip themselves apart with it. Don't you do it."

"Yeah."

"I mean it, Tamara. Don't go that route."

". . . Matter that much to you, what I do or think?"

"Bet your ass it matters."

A little more silence. Then, "Bet *your* ass you better call next time anything like this goes down. Otherwise you can get some other poor fool to do your scut work."

"Scut work, hell. I can't get along without you anymore and you know it."

"Sure. Ms. Private Eye in training."

"A good investigator in training."

"So? Do I hear a promise?"

"I promise. If there's a next time, and I damn well hope there isn't."

"Better remember that," she said. Then she said, "It wasn't just what was going on up there, you know."

"No? What else?"

"You, massuh. I was worried about *you,* all right?"

And she hung up on me. Not gently, but not too hard either.

It was one o'clock that afternoon before I finished answering the last question, signing the last official document. They let me leave then, the not-very-grateful feds and the not-too-apprecia- tive county law. I was weary, burned out, and I thought about staying over in Susanville for the rest of the day and night, as DeFalco was planning to do. But I was also fed up with this part of the state; I couldn't talk myself into spending another night in the Corner. I needed to be home, to be with Kerry—had never needed either so badly.

So I went ahead and made the long, long drive to San Fran- cisco, stopping once for gas and once to feed my hunger. Thoughts and memories rode with me, and the worst of them was the sound of Helen McDowell's tearful voice on the phone, and the last hollow words she'd said to me: "Thank you. You did all that anybody could've done—thank you." The last hour and a half of the drive seemed as interminable as the official questions, but then it ended, as all things end, and I was home. And Kerry was there for me, as she always is when I need her most.

There was quiet talk, and holding, and lovemaking, and after- ward, lying close together, hands clasped, in her big, warm bed, I could feel the fatigue and sadness and anger easing, some of the darkness of recent events burning away. Love heals much more quickly than time does. It wouldn't be long, not too long, before all that had happened in Creekside took on a distance, a remoteness, and the details faded, and it all became no more than an incident, one more difficult case among dozens of other difficult cases hidden away in that part of me that is walled against pain—or, anyway, walled against all but the sharp twinges stirred by an occasional memory. It wouldn't be long, not too long, before things were back to normal, or what passes for normal in my world.

That was what I thought then, just before I drifted off to sleep.

But I was wrong.

What made me wrong was circumstances. Direct and indirect, my actions and the actions of others known and unknown to me. The ripple effect. The old "what-if" game that could make you a little crazy, or even a lot crazy, if you played it often and long enough . . .

I was sleeping hard and restless, fighting off dreams that were all bad feeling and no substance, when Kerry woke me with a combination of words and gentle shaking. I pried one eye open. Morning. She was still in her robe, but her hair had been combed and she'd applied about half of her makeup.

"I was going to let you sleep until I left for work," she said, "but there's a call for you."

Groggily I squinted at the bedside clock. Seven-fifteen. "This early? Who is it?"

"Joe DeFalco. He sounds upset."

"What's the matter?"

"He said he'd tell you."

I rolled out of bed, aching and stiff, eliciting an indignant yowl from Shameless, who had been sleeping butted up against my leg, and found my robe and slippers and hobbled out to the phone.

"What's up, Joe?"

"I've got news. Bad." He sounded upset, all right. As upset as I'd ever heard him. Emotion thickened his voice, gave it a phlegmy quality.

"Now what's going on up there?"

"Nothing. It's not about the Sentinels."

"What, then?"

"Sometime late last night, they're not sure just when—" He broke off, and I heard him suck in a heavy breath. "Ah, Jesus, I hate this," he said. And then, "Night-beat *Chron* reporter at the Hall of Justice just got word to me. Patrol car found him a couple of hours ago, out by Islais Creek."

"Found who? Joe, you're not making sense—"

"Eberhardt," he said. "Eberhardt's dead. Shot in his car, once through the head with a .44 Magnum."